Enid Blyton

THE POOR
LITTLE SPARROW

and other animal stories

Illustrated by
Edgar Hodges
and Joyce Johnson

World International Publishing Limited
Manchester

Copyright © 1991 Darrell Waters Limited.
This compilation 1991.
These stories were first published in Sunny Stories and Enid
Blyton's Magazine between 1928 and 1959.
Enid Blyton's signature is a Registered Trade Mark of
Darrell Waters Limited.

All rights reserved.

Published in Great Britain by World International
Publishing Limited,
An Egmont Company, Egmont House, PO Box 111,
Great Ducie Street,
Manchester M60 3BL.
Printed in Italy.

No part of this publication may be reproduced, stored in a
retrieval system, or transmitted, in any form or by any
means, electronic, mechanical, photocopying, recording or
otherwise, without the prior permission of the publishers.

British Library Cataloguing in Publication Data
Blyton, Enid 1897–1968
The poor little sparrow and other animal stories.
I. Title
823. 912 [J]

ISBN 0–7498–0300–2

Cover illustration by Robin Lawrie

Contents

Enid Blyton

Enid Blyton was born in London in 1897. Her childhood was spent in Beckenham, Kent, and as a child she began to write poems, stories and plays. She trained to be a teacher but she devoted her whole life to being a children's author. Her first book was a collection of poems for children, published in 1922. In 1926 she began to write a weekly magazine for children called *Sunny Stories*, and it was here that many of her most popular stories and characters first appeared. The magazine was immensely popular and in 1953 it became *The Enid Blyton Magazine*.

She wrote more than 600 books for children and many of her most popular series are still published all over the world. Her books have been translated into over 30 languages. Enid Blyton died in 1968.

The poor little sparrow

Every morning Ronnie and Sylvia put out crumbs for the birds, and a little bowl of water. The birds always knew when the children were going to throw out the food, and they came flocking down to wait.

"Chirrup-chirrup!" said all the sparrows, dressed in brown.

"Tirry-lee, tirry-lee!" sang the robin in his creamy voice.

"Fizz, splutter, wheeee!" chattered the starlings in their funny voices.

"Pink, pink!" the pink-chested chaffinch shouted.

"Aren't they lovely?" said the children, as they threw out the crumbs and some crusts from the toast. "They really are friendly little things."

The children knew all the birds, though it was difficult to tell one sparrow from another. They knew the smallest one of all, though, because he had one white feather in his tail, and that made him look rather odd.

One day the little sparrow flew down with the others, but it couldn't seem to stand on the ground properly. It fell over – then tried to stand upright again – and then fell over again.

"Look at the poor little sparrow," said Sylvia, who was very tender-hearted. "What's the matter with it? It can't stand."

"It's hurt its leg," said Ronnie. "Oh, Sylvia – I believe its leg is broken. Can you see?"

Sylvia went slowly closer to the birds. They did not mind, for they trusted the two children. "Oh, Ronnie, you are right," she said. "Its leg is broken in two. Whatever are we to do?"

Now the poor little sparrow had that

morning been caught by a cat, but had managed to get away. Its little leg had been broken, and the tiny creature did not know why it could not stand properly, nor why it was in pain. It had joined the other birds as usual for its breakfast, but it could not eat, for it felt too ill.

Suddenly it fell right over and lay on the grass. Its eyes closed. Sylvia picked it up gently and put its soft little head against her cheek.

"Poor little sparrow," she said. "It says in the Bible that God sees every sparrow that falls, so I expect He saw you too, and hoped I would pick you up. Well, I have – but I don't know what to do to make you better."

But her mother knew. As soon as she saw the little bird she took out the old, empty, canary's cage and put the sparrow on to some clean sand at the bottom of the cage.

"It has had a shock," said their mother. "It will come awake soon, and will be all right. Oh, look! Its leg is broken!"

"How can we mend it?" asked Sylvia, almost in tears.

"Well," said her mother, "if *we* break our legs the doctor sets the bone in the right position, and then ties it to something that will keep it straight till the broken bone joins together and grows properly again. What can we tie to the sparrow's tiny leg to keep it straight?"

"A match – a match!" cried Ronnie, and he emptied some out of a box.

"That's a good idea," said Mummy. She gently picked up the sparrow, whose eyes were still closed, and laid it on the table. Then she tried to set the poor little leg straight. With strands of silk she fastened the straight matchstick to the thin, small leg. It looked very strange – but now the broken leg was straight again.

"Oh, Mummy," said Sylvia joyfully, "you've done it so nicely. When the bone joins again, the leg will be quite all right, won't it?"

"I hope so," said her mother, putting the sparrow into the cage and shutting the door. "We shall keep the tiny thing in here, and feed it until the leg is quite right, and then it shall go free again."

When the sparrow opened its eyes, it was surprised to find itself in a cage. Its leg still felt strange, but it now no longer fell over, because the matchstick supported it. The little bird flew to a perch and chirruped.

Ronnie gave it some seed. Sylvia gave it a mixture of potato and breadcrumbs, and the sparrow was simply delighted. It had a little dish of water for a bath and another dish to drink from, set at the side of the big cage. At first it fluttered its wings against the bars of the cage to get out, for it hated not being free. But, as it still did not feel very well, it soon gave up struggling and sat contentedly on a

perch, feeding and bathing whenever it wanted to.

The leg healed quickly. It was marvellous to see it. The skin joined nicely, and the broken bones seemed to grow together at once.

"I think we might let our little sparrow fly away now," said their mother one day. "I am sure his leg is all right."

"Are you going to take the matchstick off now?" asked Sylvia.

"Yes," said her mother. So she took hold of the half-frightened bird, and carefully and gently took away the silk binding from the leg and match. The match fell off – and the little leg was as straight and strong as ever.

"We've mended its leg! We've mended its leg!" shouted the children in delight. "You aren't a poor little sparrow any more. Fly away, fly away!"

The sparrow gave a chirrup and flew straight out of the window. How glad it was to be out of the cage! It flew into the trees, and chirruped so loudly that all the other sparrows came round to hear what it had to say.

Now you would not think that a small sparrow could possibly help the children in anything, would you? And yet, a few weeks later, a very strange thing happened.

Ronnie and Sylvia had some glass marbles, the prettiest things you ever saw. They were blue and green and pink, and had white lines curving through them. Ronnie and Sylvia were very proud of them, for they had belonged to their daddy.

"You can't get marbles like these nowadays," said Daddy. "Take care of them."

Well, Ronnie and Sylvia took them to play with in the fields, and there they met David, a big rough boy whom none of the children liked. When he saw the marbles he came up.

"Give me those," he said, "and I'll give you these reins of mine."

"No, thank you," said Ronnie, gathering his marbles up quickly. But he wasn't quick enough. David grabbed some of them and ran off laughing. Sylvia and Ronnie went after him.

"They are *our* marbles!" shouted Ronnie. "Give them back, David!"

"I'll put them somewhere and you take them," called back David – and what do you suppose he did with them? Why, the horrid boy dropped them all into a hole in a tree. Then he ran off, giggling.

Ronnie and Sylvia ran to the tree. They tried to slip their small hands into the hole but they couldn't. The hole was too small.

"We can't get our marbles out," said Sylvia. "They're gone. Oh, that horrid boy!"

"Chirrup!" said a cheerful little voice nearby. The children looked up. It was their little sparrow. They knew it was the same one because of the white feather in his tail.

"I wish *you* could get our marbles," sighed Ronnie. "Your foot is quite small enough to go into the hole, Sparrow."

"Chirrup!" said the sparrow – and what do you think he did? Why, he flew to the hole, and instead of putting in his foot, he put the whole of himself in. Yes, he quite disappeared into that little hole – but not for long.

He popped up again, head-first – and in his beak he held a green marble. He dropped it on to the ground and disappeared into the hole once more. Up he came, with a blue marble this time. The children were so astonished that they didn't even pick up the marbles.

The little sparrow fetched every single marble out of the hole before he flew off with a last cheerful chirrup. Then the children picked them up, and went racing home to tell their mother the strange and lovely happening.

"How very extraordinary!" she said. "It must be put into a story, for everyone will love to read about the poor little sparrow that did such a kind thing. It just shows what friends we can make, if only we are kind to even the smallest things."

So here is the story – and I do hope you enjoyed it.

Muddy-One and Pranky

"There goes old Muddy-One!" said the big water-snail. "Look out, you young frogs."

The little frogs swam up to the top of the pond at once. They were all afraid of Muddy-One. He was a large, ugly grub who lurked in the mud, and was always hungry.

Curly-Shell, the snail, wasn't at all afraid of Muddy-One. He had only to curl himself up in his hard shell whenever he spied the big grub, and nobody could harm him then. But most of the other creatures in the pond were afraid of the ugly old grub.

Pranky, the water-pixie, teased him dreadfully. He was a naughty little

mischief, very quick and cheeky, and the names he called Muddy-One made all the snails and fishes laugh.

Muddy-One had been in the pond for a very long time. He had been small at first, but now he was big. He crawled about in the mud, and across his face he put a curious claw, which could shoot out and catch any little water creature in its pincers.

He didn't like being teased by Pranky. "I can't help being ugly," he would say. "I didn't make myself. If I could have made myself I would have given myself beautiful wings, and a gleaming body, and I wouldn't live down here in the slimy mud, but up in the sunshine. Sometimes I crawl up a water-plant and look out of the water. Up there is a lovely world of light and warmth. I wish I belonged to it."

"Well, you don't! An ugly creature like you wouldn't be allowed to live up in the bright sunshine," said Pranky, and he poked the grub with a bit of stick. "How lazy you are! Stir yourself! Gallop round the pond a bit."

But Muddy-One wasn't very gallopy. He didn't like being poked with a stick, and he was angry with the unkind little pixie. But that only made Pranky call him ruder names than ever; so in the end Muddy-One buried himself deep down in the slime and tried to hide.

"He's ashamed of himself, and I don't wonder," cried Pranky, poking his stick into the mud. "What a pity somebody doesn't eat him. I'll find a big fish one day, Muddy-One, and send him along to eat you."

"You shouldn't tease Muddy-One so," said the big water-snail. "He doesn't do you any harm. You're unkind."

Then Pranky swam to the snail and tried to pull him out of his shell. But he couldn't. So he wrote a rude sentence on the snail's shell and left him. He put "I am a poor old slow-coach" all over the snail's shell, and the snail couldn't think why everyone who met him laughed.

Pranky was just as much at home in the air as in the water. He was lucky, for he could run and swim and fly. He was a fine-looking pixie too, and he knew it. He often used a shining dewdrop as a mirror, and looked at himself proudly in it.

One day the Princess Melisande thought she would give a party. Now, she lived high up on a hill above the clouds, so it was plain that every guest would have to fly there.

"I shall get my Peacock-butterfly to take me," said Jinky the fairy.

"I'm going on Zoom the bumble-bee," said Tippy the goblin.

"I've got my lovely Tiger-moth," said Twink the elf.

"What are *you* going on, Pranky?" asked Jinky.

"I shall ask the bluebottle to fly to Princess Melisande's with me," said Pranky. "He's such a lovely colour."

But he couldn't ride the bluebottle because somebody saw it crawling with dirty feet over a baby's bottle, and the baby's mother chased it far away.

"He's a dirty, horrid bluebottle fly," said the mother. "He'll make the baby ill."

So there was no bluebottle for the pixie to ride on. He *was* upset. "Can I ride on Zoom with you?" he asked Tippy.

"No. He says you once sewed up the end of a foxglove flower when he had crawled inside, and he couldn't get out," said Tippy. "He doesn't like you."

"Well, can I come on your butterfly?" Pranky asked Jinky.

"No, you can't. He isn't strong enough to carry two of us," said Jinky. "Why don't you get a dragonfly? He'd be very strong indeed, and very beautiful too. He would fly so fast that you'd be at the Princess's in no time!"

"Oooh, yes! – I'd love a dragonfly," said Pranky, thinking how very grand he would feel riding such a lovely creature. "But I haven't seen any yet. Where can I get one?"

"You'd better go and ask old Mother Wimple," said Jinky. "She knows all the insects well. She's always mending their wings for them when they get torn. She could get you a dragonfly, I expect. But be polite to her, Pranky, because she's got a hot temper."

Pranky flew off. He soon came to where Mother Wimple lived. She had a tiny house by the pond, and she was sitting outside it, busily patching the torn wing of a butterfly.

"Mother Wimple, I'm going to Princess Melisande's party," said Pranky, sitting down beside her. "And her palace is so high above the clouds that I've got to get some insect to take me. I want a dragonfly. Could you get me one, please?"

"You're very polite all of a sudden," said old Mother Wimple, who had not heard very good tales of Pranky.

"You're one of those people who have very good manners when they want something, and can be very rude when they don't, aren't you?"

"Oh, *no!*" said Pranky, going rather red. "No, I'm very well behaved, Mother Wimple. Please do tell me if you can get me a dragonfly."

"When is the party?" asked Mother Wimple.

"Tomorrow afternoon," said Pranky.

"Come back an hour before you have to set off for the party, and I'll have here the finest dragonfly you ever saw," said Mother Wimple.

Pranky flew off in the greatest delight. He was back in good time the next day, but he couldn't see any dragonfly.

"Be patient," said Mother Wimple. "You'll see him soon. Ah – here he comes."

She pointed to a water-plant whose stem came right up out of the pond. Up it was crawling the ugly old grub,

Muddy-One. Pranky stared at him and then he stared at Mother Wimple.

"Why – that's no dragonfly – that's only ugly old Muddy-One!" he said.

"Oh, you know him, do you?" said Mother Wimple. "Well now, you watch and see what is going to happen to him. You'll see something marvellous."

Pranky watched. Old Muddy-One crawled right out of the water, and clung to the stem of the water-plant, enjoying the hot sunshine.

Then, to the pixie's enormous surprise, the ugly old grub split his skin right down his back!

"Gracious goodness, look at that!" said Pranky. "He's split himself. Has he eaten too much? I always told him he'd burst if he was so greedy."

"Be quiet," said Mother Wimple. "Now look – he's split even farther."

Pranky watched in surprise. He saw that the ugly old grub was trying to creep out of his own skin. How extraordinary!

But what a different creature came out of the old skin! He had a long slender body that gleamed blue green. He had crumpled wings. He had enormous eyes that shone in the sun, and six weak legs that clung to the water-plant for safety.

"Why – Muddy-One's got wings," cried Pranky. "Look – he's spreading them out in the sun to dry them. They are long and lovely, and look at his beautiful blue-green body and eyes. Oh, Mother Wimple, he's not an ugly water-grub any longer, he's a most *beautiful* dragonfly. It's magic, it's magic! Oh, how clever of you to make a dragonfly come out of Muddy's old skin."

"I didn't," said Mother Wimple. "All dragonflies live down in the mud as grubs for a long time. But when the right time comes, they creep up into the sunshine, take off their old skin, and dart up into the air – bright, beautiful dragonflies!"

"Oh, I shall love to ride him," cried Pranky. Mother Wimple called to the dragonfly as he sat sunning his wings

"Swift-One! Come here and take this pixie to Princess Melisande's party."

The dragonfly flew over to Mother Wimple and soared round her head, gleaming in the sun. Pranky stood up in delight.

"Let me ride you, let me ride you!" he cried.

Swift-One the dragonfly flew just out of reach. "What! Let you, a rude and ill-mannered pixie, ride me, the swiftest dragonfly in the world? Certainly not! I haven't forgotten how you teased me and the names you called me, you horrid little pixie!"

"That's not the way to talk, Swift-One," said Mother Wimple sternly. "I have promised Pranky that he shall ride you. Come down, so that he may get on your back."

Swift-One darted down, and Pranky leapt on to his back. The dragonfly soared high in the air at such a pace that Pranky's breath was almost taken away. But then Swift-One began to play tricks.

He stopped suddenly in mid-air, and Pranky almost shot over his head. He flew upside-down, and Pranky nearly fell off. He darted down to the surface of the pond and made the pixie get his feet wet. He teased Pranky just as much as Pranky had once teased him, down in the pond.

Then he turned over and over and over in the air, and at last, the pixie, too giddy to hold on any longer, fell off and flew down to the ground, landing beside Mother Wimple with a bump.

He began to cry when he saw the dragonfly darting away at top speed. Mother Wimple laughed.

"It serves you right," she said. "I thought he would play a few tricks on you if he had the chance. Cry, Pranky, cry! Perhaps you will learn now not to make fun of ugly, slow creatures.

You never know when they are going to change into beautiful, swift flying things that will tip you off their backs."

"I c-c-c-can't go to the party now," wept Pranky. "Tippy's gone by on his butterfly, and Jinky's gone on Zoom the bumble-bee, but I've got no one to take *me*!"

He went home, very sorry for himself. And all that August and September he had to keep a sharp look out for Swift-One, because the dragonfly flew down to tease the bad little pixie whenever he saw him.

Have you seen Swift-One, the dragonfly? Look out for him. He's beautiful.

The tale of Jig and Jog

One day Jig and Jog, the two brownies who lived in Hollyhock Cottage, made up their minds to give a party.

"It shall be a birthday party," said Jig. "Then everyone will bring us presents. Won't that be nice, Jog?"

"Yes!" said Jog, rubbing his horny little hands in glee. "Ha! Presents of cakes! And sweets! And all kinds of exciting things!"

"We will give our party on November the fourteenth," said Jig. "We will send out the invitation cards now."

"Who shall come to the party?" said Jog.

"Well, we will ask Prickles the

hedgehog," said Jig. "He makes beautiful cakes. He might bring us one. We will put on our invitation cards that it is a birthday party. Then he will know he must bring a present."

"Who else shall come?" asked Jog.

"Well, Slinky the snake would be a good person to ask," said Jig, "and so would Slow-One the toad; and his cousin, Hoppity, the frog. Oh, and don't you think we could ask that bird who plays hide-and-seek so well – what's his name, now?"

"You mean the cuckoo," said Jog. "Yes, we will ask him too; and we will ask Dozy the little dormouse, for he is a generous fellow, and might even bring us a present each, instead of one between us."

The two brownies made out their list and then wrote out their invitation cards.

"Please come to a birthday party at Hollyhock Cottage on November the fourteenth, at four o'clock", they wrote on each card. Then they posted all the cards in the pillar-box at the end of the road, and waited for the answers.

The postman, Floppy the rabbit, took the cards and went to deliver them. He knew where Prickles the hedgehog lived, in a cosy hole in the sunny bankside of the hedge. He slipped the card into the hole. He knew where Slinky the snake lived too – in the old hollow tree in the middle of the wood. He climbed up and dropped the card down into the hole. He was a very good postman.

Then Floppy took Slow-One's card, and went to a big stone by the pond. He knew Slow-One the toad lived there. He pushed the card under the stone and left it. Hoppity the frog lived in the pond. Floppy waited until a stickleback came up to the top of the water and asked him to take the card to Hoppity. The fish caught the card neatly in its mouth and swam off with it.

"Now there's the card for the cuckoo,"

said Floppy Rabbit to himself. "Well, he was always sitting in that big beech tree, calling 'cuckoo' to everyone, so I'll put his card there. He is sure to see it if he sits there again."

Floppy had only one card left now – and that was for Dozy the dormouse. Floppy knew quite well where Dozy was living. He was in a cosy hole deep down in the roots of the big fir tree at the edge of the wood, not far from Floppy's own burrow. So, being a sensible rabbit, Floppy left that card till last, stuffed it into Dozy's hole, and then slipped into his own burrow for a rest and a cup of carrot tea.

Jig and Jog waited impatiently for the answers to their invitations. But none came! It was most extraordinary. Jig and Jog were puzzled. And then Jig thought he knew why. They had not put on the cards that they wanted an answer! So perhaps all their guests had thought they need not reply. Well, it didn't matter. The two brownies felt quite sure they would all turn up at the party on the right day – each bringing a very nice present!

They began to get ready for the party. They each had a new suit made, a red one for Jig and a blue one for Jog. They made a batch of chocolate cakes and a batch of ginger ones. They made strawberry jam sandwiches. They put out a clean cloth and arranged chairs all round their small table.

"We said four o'clock on the invitation cards," said Jig, when the day came. "It's half-past three now. Are we quite, quite ready, Jog?"

"Well, we've put on our new suits, and we've laid the table and put out the cakes and sandwiches and arranged the chairs," said Jog. "Yes, we are quite ready. I wonder who will come first!"

"And I wonder what everyone will bring us," said Jig. "It's a good thing we told everyone it was a birthday party, so that we can get presents."

Four o'clock came – but nobody

walked up the garden path. How strange! Quarter-past four and still no guests! Half-past four – five o'clock! Where could everyone be? There were the cakes and the sandwiches – but no guests to eat them. Jig and Jog looked as if they were going to cry!

They went down the garden path and looked up and down the road. Only Dame Chippy was there, coming along with the washing. When she saw their sad faces she stopped.

"What's the matter?" she asked.

"Well," said Jig mournfully, "we sent out invitations to Prickles, Slinky, Slow-One, Hoppity, the cuckoo and Dozy to come to a birthday party today – and nobody's come – and we shan't get any presents."

"Don't you know that you never tell anyone a party is a *birthday* party?" said Dame Chippy, shocked. "Why, that's just asking for presents, and nobody with good manners does that. It serves you right that nobody has come."

"But *why* haven't they come?" wailed Jog.

"If you think hard you'll know," said Dame Chippy, with a grin.

Jig and Jog thought hard – but they didn't know. Do you? Dame Chippy had to tell them.

"You are two silly creatures," she said. "Don't you know that Prickles the hedgehog always finds a hole for himself in the winter and sleeps the cold days away? Don't you know that Slinky the snake hates the cold and hides in a hollow tree fast asleep until the spring comes? And Slow-One the toad is never awake in the winter, sillies! He is sound asleep under his big stone – and his cousin, Hoppity the frog, is hidden in the mud at the bottom of the pond! As for the cuckoo, he has left the land months ago. He always goes south for the winter to find warmth and food."

"What about Dozy?" asked Jig in a small voice.

"He sleeps more soundly than any of

them!" said Dame Chippy. "He's snoring in the roots of the old fir tree! Well, well, well – no wonder you have no guests and no birthday presents! It serves you right for being so stupid and greedy!"

"Oh, all our cards were wasted, and all our cakes will be wasted too," wept Jig and Jog in dismay.

"Your cakes needn't be wasted!" said Dame Chippy. "I'll come in and eat them for you!"

And so she did – but Jig and Jog weren't a bit pleased. What sillies they were, weren't they?

A lame duck and a stile

"I'm taking my doll for a walk, Mummy," said Amanda. "I've put her into her pram and tucked her up. We shall just go across the fields and back."

"You won't be able to take your pram over the stile," said Mummy, "so don't try."

"I won't," said Amanda. "I'll just walk as far as the stile, then I'll turn back. That will be a nice walk for Rosebud."

Rosebud was her doll, a small, lovely little thing, lying in the pram with her eyes shut. She aways shut them when she lay down. Mother said she wished babies would do that too. It would be so nice if they all went to sleep as soon as they were put down in prams or cots!

Rosebud opened her eyes when she sat up. She had blue eyes and golden hair. Amanda loved her very much. She liked taking her for walks in the pram. She often talked to her as she went along.

She talked to her that morning, although Rosebud was asleep, with her eyes shut.

"It's a lovely sunny day," said Amanda. "The buttercups are out all over the field, Rosebud. They are brushing against the wheels of the pram and making them all yellow."

Rosebud said nothing. She kept her eyes shut.

"The birds are singing," said Amanda. "I can hear them. Sit up and listen, Rosebud. It would do you good to be awake now."

She sat Rosebud up. Rosebud opened her blue eyes and looked at Amanda. She was a very smiley doll, and her smile showed two rows of tiny white teeth. Amanda sometimes tried to clean Rosebud's tiny teeth, but it wasn't easy.

"Now you can see the buttercups, and hear the birds singing," said Amanda. Then she stopped talking and looked puzzled.

"What's that noise?" she said. "It sounds like a very loud quacking!"

It was. "QUACK, QUACK, QUACK!" went the noise. "QUACK, QUACK, QUACK!"

"There aren't any ducks near here, surely?" said Amanda. "They all swim on the pond at the farm. Rosebud, we had better find out if it *is* a duck."

They went on down the path across the buttercup field. The noise grew louder. Amanda came to the stile and stopped.

The quacking seemed to come from the other side. She peeped over the stile. She was surprised to see a large white duck there, looking up at her out of bright eyes.

"Hallo!" said Amanda, rather startled. "What are you quacking for?"

"QUACK!" said the duck, and put its head through an opening under the stile.

"I see. You want to get over that stile," said Amanda. "Well, why don't you?"

"Quack, quack," said the duck, in a sad sort of voice.

Then Amanda saw that it had a bad foot. It had webbed skin between its toes to help it when it swam – but the webbing on one foot was torn. Now it was lame and could hardly get along on its one good foot.

"Poor thing! You can't get over the stile!" said Amanda, in pity. "I'll help you over. Mummy is always saying something about helping lame ducks over a stile, but I never thought *I* should do that! I thought it was just a saying that meant helping people in trouble."

But this time it was real. There was a real lame duck, trying to get over a real stile, and Amanda was there to help it.

She climbed over the stile, and tried to push the duck through, over the bottom bar. It was difficult because the duck didn't seem to think that Amanda was trying to help it. It gave her a peck.

"Oh, don't do that when I'm trying to help you!" said Amanda. "That's not kind. Now – one more push – and over you go, poor lame duck!"

This time the duck did go over the stile and, much to its surprise, found itself on the other side. This was where it wanted to be.

It had swum out of the pond and down the stream. Then it had caught its foot on some sharp stones, and climbed on to the bank because its foot hurt it too much to swim. It thought it would go home by the fields. But it hadn't been able to get over the stile.

Now it was over. It looked up at Amanda and said "Quack!" She thought

perhaps it meant "Thank you." It began to waddle slowly along the path, which led to the farm where its pond was. But it couldn't even waddle properly now. Its foot hurt it too much.

It sank down among the buttercups and gave a most doleful quack. Amanda looked at it in alarm.

"Can't you walk? You ought to get back to the farm and have your leg seen to. Try again."

The duck tried again, but once more it fell over. Amanda couldn't bear it. She wondered what to do.

"I know!" she said. "I'll wheel you in my pram. I once read a story about a little girl who wheeled a lost lamb home in her pram. So I don't see why I shouldn't wheel a lame duck."

She bent down to pick up the big, heavy duck. It pecked her hands.

"Don't!" said Amanda. "I'm only trying to help you! I can't leave you here. The fox might get you! He lives about these fields."

She bent down again, and again the duck pecked her and made a nasty sound in its throat. Amanda didn't know what to do. What an ungrateful duck!

She had one last try. She picked up the big duck and popped it into her pram! It pecked her again and tried to strike her with its wing. Amanda felt rather hurt.

"You're unkind," she said. "Oh, do keep still! You're sitting on poor Rosebud!"

The duck wriggled about in the pram, and then it pecked Rosebud's nose! Amanda was really cross.

"Now look here, Duck, I've done a lot for you, and I'm taking you home in Rosebud's pram. You've quacked at me and pecked me, and hit me with your wings – but you're *not* going to peck Rosebud! Sit still!"

After that the duck did sit still. It squatted comfortably down in the pram, leaving Rosebud just enough room, and quacked no more. It closed its eyes.

"Perhaps it likes being in the pram," thought Amanda, and wheeled it carefully along the path. She came to the farm and called to the farmer's wife.

"I've got one of your ducks in my pram. It has hurt its foot."

"Bless us all! Fancy wheeling it back here, you kind little thing!" cried Mrs Straw, and hurried to get the duck. It gave Amanda one last peck.

"It doesn't like me," said Amanda, almost in tears. "I only tried to help it. It keeps pecking me."

"Only because it is in pain, dear," said Mrs Straw, and took the duck away to see to its foot. "Thank you for bringing it home."

Amanda went home with Rosebud to tell her mother about the duck. "It wasn't a nice duck," she said. "It didn't like me, even when I tried to help it. It never even quacked a thank you."

Amanda was sad. She went to her pram to take Rosebud out – and then she got a surprise!

In the pram lay a big greenish-grey duck's egg! Amanda stared at it in the greatest astonishment. She picked it up and ran to her mother.

"Mummy! The duck's laid me an egg! It must have liked me after all! Look!"

"What a beauty!" said Mummy. "That's the best reward the duck could give you, isn't it? You can have it for your breakfast."

"But I don't like ducks' eggs," said Amanda. "I had one at Auntie's once and it tasted funny. I don't want to eat it, Mummy . . ."

"Well – shall we give it to Henny-Penny to sit on?" said Mummy. "She has ten of her own eggs to sit on, and she won't mind if we add this duck's egg to her batch. Then maybe you will have a little duckling of your own!"

Amanda thought that was a fine idea. She put the warm duck's egg with

Henny-Penny's big batch of brown eggs. Henny-Penny, the brown hen, didn't seem to mind a bit.

And do you know, out of that greenish-grey duck's egg came the dearest little yellow duckling you ever saw! Henny-Penny sat on her eggs for some weeks, and ten of them hatched into yellow chicks – and one into the duckling!

"It's *my* duckling!" cried Amanda, in delight. "My very own. You shall be my pet, little duckling. I shall call you Quack!"

I saw Quack yesterday, and Amanda told me this story. She thought you might like to hear it too.

"I helped a lame duck over a stile!" she said, "and that's how I got a duckling for my own. I *am* a lucky girl, aren't I?"

The ugly old toad

Once upon a time a big old toad wanted to cross the road to get to a pond he knew on the other side. He couldn't jump high and quickly like his cousin the frog. He could only do small hops, or crawl, but he set off valiantly, hoping to get across the road before anything came along.

He was almost across when a horse and cart came down the lane. Clippitty-cloppitty, clippitty-cloppitty went the horse's hoofs, and the old toad heard them. He tried to hop away quickly, but one of the horse's hoofs trod on his back leg. Almost at once the horse lifted his hoof again and went on, not knowing that he had crushed the foot of the toad.

"Oh!" groaned the toad to himself, crawling to the side of the road, dragging his hurt foot behind him. "What a bit of bad luck! I can hardly walk now. How my foot is hurting me!"

He was in such pain that he could not go any farther. He squatted by the side of the road, hoping that his foot would soon get better. But it didn't.

He tried again to crawl, but his foot hurt him too much, so he lay there, half-hidden by a tuft of grass, hoping that no enemy would come by.

The big rat ran by and stopped when he saw the toad. "Aha! Dinner for me!" thought the rat, knowing that the toad was hurt. He ran up to the toad and snapped at him.

The toad still could not crawl away, but he had a good trick to play on the rat. He oozed out an evil-smelling, horrible-tasting liquid all over his back. When the rat tried to bite him, he got his mouth full of the nasty stuff.

"Horrible!" said the rat, and stood staring at the toad with his mouth open, trying to let the nasty-tasting stuff drip out of his mouth. "Horrible! I wouldn't have *you* for my dinner for anything!"

He ran off, and the toad sat still, glad to be rid of him. Then he heard footsteps coming down the lane, and he shrank back into the grass, trying to look like a brown clod of earth. He really did look like one.

Soon a boy came up, whistling. He almost trod on the toad, but he did not see him and went whistling on. He thought the old toad was just a lump of earth.

He stayed still, hoping that his foot would stop hurting. But the horse's hoof had been hard and heavy – it was a wonder it had not cut the toad's foot right off.

Then the toad heard more footsteps – lighter ones this time. He crouched down again, but this time the passer-by was sharper-eyed than the boy.

"Ooh! A toad!" said a voice, and the toad, looking up cautiously, saw a little girl gazing down at him. She wrinkled her nose in disgust.

"Nasty creature! I can't bear toads! Ugly thing with your pimply back and your creepy-crawly ways! I don't like you a bit!"

The toad crouched very still. He was afraid. This little girl might stamp on him – children were sometimes very cruel to creatures like him. But he couldn't help being an ugly old toad – he was born like that.

However, the little girl did not stamp on him. She wasn't cruel. She did think the toad was ugly, and she didn't like him much, but she wasn't going to be unkind.

"I don't like ugly creatures," she said to the toad. "I couldn't bear to touch you. Oooh, that *would* be horrid! It would make me feel ill."

The toad was sad. He wished he had been born a butterfly or a bird. Then perhaps the little girl would have liked him. But you had to be what you were born to be – there wasn't any help for it.

Then suddenly the little girl saw the toad's foot. It was all crushed and flattened. She stared at it in horror.

"Toad! Your foot is squashed to bits! Is it hurting you? Oh, how did that happen? Did someone tread on you?"

The toad still crouched flat. He knew the little girl wouldn't tread on him now, but he was still afraid. She looked at him, sad because of his foot.

"Oh, I can't leave you here like this," she said. "I'm sorry I said all those unkind things now. I didn't know you were hurt. I think I had better take you home to my mother – she will know what to do with your foot."

The toad didn't want to be taken home. He wanted to be left alone in peace. The little girl was wondering how to carry him.

"Although I am very sorry for you, I simply *can't* touch you," she said. "I can't! I should drop you if I touched you. You see, I don't like toads."

Then she thought of using her handkerchief. She would wrap the toad in that and carry him by taking hold of the four corners of the hanky. Then she would not need to touch him at all.

So to the toad's surprise and fright, she dropped her hanky over him, rolled him gently into it, and picked him up in the hanky. She carried him by taking hold of the four corners, but she didn't even like doing that!

She took him home. The toad did not wriggle or struggle, because it hurt his foot too much. He just lay in the hanky, very miserable, wondering what was going to happen to him.

The little girl went in at her gate. She called to her mother. "Mummy! I've got a hurt toad. Can you do something for him?"

Her mother was very surprised. She undid the hanky and took the toad in her bare hands. She didn't mind touching any creature. She saw the hurt foot and was sorry.

"I can't do much," she said. "I will just bathe it with very weak iodine – but it's no good binding it up. The best thing you can do for him, Jenny, is to put him in a cool, shady corner of the garden, where there are plenty of flies for him to catch, and leave him to himself. Maybe the foot will heal itself."

"I don't like him much," said Jenny.

"He can't help being a toad," said her mother. "*You* might have been born a toad – and think how sad you would be if people hated you, and tried to hurt you because you happened to be ugly. That's not fair, Jenny."

"No, it isn't," said Jenny. She looked down at the toad, and he looked up at her. She saw his eyes.

"Mummy, he's got the most beautiful eyes!" she said, surprised. "Do look at them. They are like jewels in his head, gleaming as bright as copper."

"All toads have lovely eyes," said

Mummy. "They are nice creatures, Jenny, and make good pets."

"Oh, *no*, Mummy!" said Jenny, astonished. "I have never heard of a toad as a pet before!"

"There are quite a lot of things you haven't heard of!" said Mummy. "Now – I've finished bathing his foot – do you think you can possibly bring yourself to carry him in your hands to a nice bit of the garden – or do you dislike toads so much?"

Jenny felt a bit ashamed of herself. She looked down at the toad. His coppery eyes gleamed kindly at her. He looked patient and wise.

"I'll carry him," she said, and she picked him up gently in her hands. He kept quite still. Jenny took him down the garden and put him in the cool hedge behind Daddy's lettuces.

"There you are!" she said. "Stay there and catch flies. I don't know what else you eat, but there are heaps of flies here for you."

There were. The toad heard a big one buzzing just over his head. He looked at it – and then, quick as a flash, he shot out a long sticky tongue, caught the fly on the tip of it, swallowed, and looked at Jenny.

"A good meal," he seemed to say. Jenny laughed.

"You're rather nice," she said, and left him.

She forgot all about him. A week went by, then two weeks. Then Daddy came in one evening, bringing two delicious lettuces for supper.

"Good gracious!" said Mummy, pleased. "I thought you told me that all your lettuces had been eaten by slugs, Daddy. What beauties these are!"

"Ah! I've got someone to guard my lettuces for me!" said Daddy. "And a very good fellow he is, too. He never allows a single slug on my lettuce-bed now."

"Who is he?" said Jenny, puzzled.

"He's a toad," said Daddy, "a wise,

friendly, kind old toad. He lives in the hedge behind my kitchen garden, and he keeps guard over the lettuces. See how well they have grown since the old toad looked after them for me!"

"Daddy! He must be *my* toad! I forgot all about him," said Jenny, excited.

"*Your* toad? I thought you didn't like toads," said Daddy. "What do you mean?"

Jenny told him. "And we shall know if it *is* my toad by his foot," she said. "Has he got a mended foot, Daddy?"

"I didn't notice," said Daddy. "Let's go and see."

So they went to see – and there was the old toad, and behind him was his hurt foot – mended and healed now, but rather a funny shape.

"It *is* my toad!" said Jenny. "Look, he's crawling over to me, Daddy. He knows I'm the little girl who brought him home."

"Tickle his back with a grass," said Daddy. "He'll like that."

So Jenny did, and the toad liked it very much. He tried to scratch his back with one of his feet, and made Jenny laugh.

"You're a good old toad," she said. "I like you, and you shall be my pet."

He *is* her pet, and he still keeps guard over the kitchen garden. I know because I've seen him there!

The snow-white pigeon

Once upon a time there was a little girl called Isabel.

She was very fond of birds and animals, but she hadn't any of her own, not even a tortoise. So she made the wild birds her pets, and fed them every day, putting the crumbs and scraps on an old tree-stump in the garden.

One day a snow-white pigeon flew down to feed with the other birds. Isabel was surprised.

"Look, Mummy," she said. "There's a fan-tail pigeon – see its beautiful fan-like tail. I wonder where it has come from. I do wish I could have one for my own."

But Isabel's mother was very poor,

and she could not even afford the few pence for the corn that the pigeon would have to eat. So she shook her head.

"We have no money for pets," she said. "Pigeons eat corn, Isabel. That one which flew down to feed is not eating anything. It just flew down to see if there was any seed or corn there – but now that it finds none it will fly away."

The pigeon *would* have flown away – but suddenly something dreadful happened. The next-door cat came creeping along, hid behind a bush –

and then jumped out at the poor white pigeon!

"Oh! Oh!" screamed Isabel in a fright, and she rushed out at once. She scared away the cat, and ran to lift up the hurt pigeon.

One of its wings had been hurt, and it could not fly. It was very frightened, and its ruby-red eyes were shut. Isabel gently carried the pigeon to her mother.

"It will be all right in a day or two," said her mother. "It must be kept in a cage until it can fly again, or the cat will get it once more."

"I haven't a cage," said Isabel, frowning. Then she cheered up. "But, Mummy, what about that old rabbit hutch in the shed? Would that do?"

"Yes, if you clean it out," said her mother. "You can easily keep the pigeon there for a little while. We must find out whom it belongs to, and they can have their pigeon back when its wing is better."

So Isabel cleaned out the old rabbit

hutch and mended the wire in front with string. Then she set it out in the garden by the dining room window. She gently placed the hurt pigeon into the old hutch.

Her mother had washed its wing, and the pigeon had its eyes open now. It was still frightened, but it did not mind Isabel's gentle hands. It knew that the little girl loved it.

"Mummy, what shall I feed it on?" asked Isabel. "I haven't a penny for some corn."

"Run down to the farmer's wife and see if she wants any errands done," said her mother. "Maybe she would give you a handful of corn if you help her a bit."

So off went Isabel, and asked Mrs Straw, the farmer's wife, if there was any work she could do.

"Yes," said Mrs Straw at once. "You can wash all the eggs for me, ready for market. I haven't time this morning. Mind you don't break any!"

Isabel washed nearly a hundred eggs

and didn't break a single one. Mrs Straw was pleased.

"You can have three eggs to take home," she said. But Isabel looked at her shyly.

"Do you think I might have a handful of corn instead?" she asked. "I've a hurt pigeon, and I've no food for it."

"Bless the child! Of course you can take the corn!" said Mrs Straw, and she bustled off to see to her baking. Isabel ran to the corn bin and took a handful of corn. Then, holding it in her overall so that she shouldn't waste even a grain, she went slowly back home. The pigeon was simply delighted with the corn, for it was very hungry.

"Rookity-coo, rookity-coo!" it said to Isabel, and pecked up the corn as quickly as it could. By the morning there was no corn left.

"I'll have to go and do a few more jobs for Mrs Straw," said Isabel. "Then perhaps she will give me some more corn."

So off she went. Mrs Straw was pleased to see her, for the little girl was a good worker.

"Good morning," she said. "You are just in time. I've six baby lambs in the farm-garden that I am bringing up by hand. Will you heat their milk for me, put it into these babies' bottles, and then feed all the lambs, one by one?"

Well, wasn't that a lovely job to do? Isabel was delighted. She heated the milk in a big saucepan on Mrs Straw's oil-stove, and then she filled the bottles. She made them cooler for the lambs, and then went out to feed them. The long-legged creatures came frisking up to her, greedy and hungry. One by one she fed them, putting the teat of the bottle into their mouths, and letting them suck out the warm milk.

"This is a lovely thing to do," sighed Isabel happily. "Dear little lambs. I can't believe you grow into those fat old sheep!"

Mrs Straw was pleased with Isabel

for helping her again. "Take six apples home for yourself," she said. "There are some in the store-room."

Isabel would dearly have liked the apples, but she wanted some corn for the pigeon. Mrs Straw nodded and said yes, she could take another handful if she liked. So Isabel took home another handful and fed the hungry pigeon.

She looked into the cage, where the pigeon was comfortably sitting on the hay. When the fan-tail walked over to the corn, Isabel saw something on the hay.

"It's an egg," she cried, "a pretty white egg! The pigeon has laid it. Oh, I wonder if a baby pigeon will come out of it!"

She ran to tell her mother. Her mother was so surprised.

"Well, well!" she said. "Who would have thought of that?"

"I do wonder whom the pigeon belongs to," said Isabel. "They will be surprised to know that it has laid an egg."

"I have found out who the owner is,"

said her mother. "It is Miss Kennedy, down the lane. She has lost one. You can go and tell her, if you like, that you have her pigeon safely."

So off went Isabel and saw Miss Kennedy, who was a very kind lady indeed, just as fond of birds and animals as Isabel was.

"A cat hurt your pigeon," said Isabel, "so I put it into an old hutch and looked after it. I hadn't any pennies to buy corn, so I did some jobs for Mrs Straw, and she let me have some corn for the pigeon. And now it has laid an egg!"

"Well, you *have* been a kind little friend to my hurt pigeon," said Miss Kennedy. "Will you keep it for me until the egg has hatched and the baby is old enough to look after itself? Perhaps you would like to keep the baby and have it for your own pigeon? I can always give you some of my corn for it!"

Isabel was so delighted that she could hardly say thank you. To have a pigeon of her very own – one that she had

had from an egg! It was too lovely for anything.

She raced back to tell the good news to her mother. She would be pleased too, because she knew how much Isabel would love a pet of her own.

The pigeon sat day after day on its white egg. Its wing healed, but Isabel did not let it fly out, in case the cat got it again. Not until the egg was hatched and the strange little baby was old enough to see to itself did she open the hutch and let the mother pigeon fly back to Miss Kennedy's pigeon-house.

But the baby pigeon always stayed with Isabel, and grew big and white and beautiful like its mother. It had a wonderful fan-tail that it spread out when it walked. It said, "Rookity-coo, rookity-coo!" to Isabel whenever it saw her.

She has the pigeon still – and guess what she has called it! I wonder if you guessed right? Well, she called it Snow White!

The poor little owl

In the field nearby lived a little brown owl. John and Betty often saw it sitting on the telegraph wires in the dusk, when they went to bed.

"Tvit, tvit, tvit!" said the little owl to them, and the children called "Tvit, tvit!" back to it. It wasn't very big, and when it spread its wings it flew very silently indeed.

Then one evening, as John and Betty walked home, they saw the little owl disappear into a hole in an old, old willow tree.

"I guess it has got its nest there!" said John in excitement. "I wonder if there will be any baby owls. We must watch and see."

But before they knew, a sad thing happened to the little owl. It went to drink from the pond one night, overbalanced, fell into the water and couldn't get out! So in the morning John and Betty found that it was drowned, and they were very sad.

"Oh, John – what about the baby owls, if there are any in the tree?" said Betty in tears. "There won't be anyone to feed them. They will starve to death, poor things."

John spoke to the gardener about the nest he was sure was in the old willow tree. "Couldn't you look and see if there are any baby owls there?" he said. "We don't want them to starve, you know."

"I'm not going after any owls," said the gardener at once. "Dangerous creatures they are, with their sharp claws! My goodness, even a baby owl can get its claws into you so hard that you can't get them out."

"Oh," said John. He went away, but he kept on and on thinking about the owls. He felt sure they were hungry and unhappy.

"Betty, there must be *some* way of getting them out," he said. "Do think. You're clever at thinking."

So Betty thought. "Well," she said, "if their claws are so sharp and strong that they can dig right into your hand and not let it go, what about letting down something into the nest – a handkerchief, perhaps – and letting them dig their claws into that. Then all we need to do is to draw up the handkerchief and the owls will come too!"

"Marvellous idea!" cried John. And so it was. Betty borrowed a big old silk hanky from Daddy's drawer, and the two children went to the old willow tree. They climbed up it and came to the hole, which went deep into a thick branch of the tree.

A faint hissing noise came up from the hole. "Goodness – is there a snake in there?" said Betty.

"No! Owls do hiss, you know," said John. "Now, Betty – where's the hanky? Hand it over."

John took the hanky and let one end slowly down into the hole. There were two baby owls in the tree. They turned themselves over so that their clawed feet were on top – and how they attacked that silk hanky! They dug their feet into it and their claws caught in the silk.

"Got them nicely!" shouted John, and

he pulled up the hanky. There were the two fluffy baby owls holding on to it for all they were worth! John popped them into a box he had brought with him, shut the lid, and then switched his torch on to see the nest.

"There isn't really any nest," he called to Betty, "just a few shavings from the hole, that's all. But wait a minute – what's this?"

The light of his torch had shone on to something red. John put his hand into the hole and felt what it was. It seemed to be a little bag of some sort. He pulled at it – and it came out. It was heavy.

"Betty! The owl had made her nest on top of this little bag!" cried John. "Look – it's got the name of the bank on it. I do believe it's the bag of gold that a thief stole from the bank messenger last winter! He must have hidden it here and then forgotten where the hiding place was!"

"Goodness!" said Betty, as John

opened the little red bag and a whole
heap of shining golden coins winked up
at them. "What a lot of money! Come
and tell Mummy."

Well, that was a most exciting
afternoon. The children had two baby
owls for pets, and a bag of gold to
give back to the bank! And what
do you think? The bank manager
gave the children one of the pieces of
gold!

"That's your reward," he said. "Buy
what you like with it."

So what do you think they bought with the money? They went to the shops and bought a marvellous cage in which to bring up their two pet owls! It was painted blue outside, and had red perches inside, and was very grand and big indeed.

"You can keep your little owls there and bring them up in safety till they are big enough to fly away and look after themselves," said their mother. "You must feed them well, give them fresh water, and clean out their cage every single day."

So they did, and soon the two owls grew tame and friendly, and sat peacefully on the children's fingers whenever they were held out to them. Betty and John were very proud of their pets, because no one else at school had owls; and even the teacher came to see them, and said what strange and curious birds they were.

"They look rather like little feathered cats!" she said. And so they did, as they sat side by side on their perches, their big golden eyes looking solemnly at the visitor.

And now they have flown away to look after themselves; but John and Betty have left the cage door open in case they might like to come back there to sleep. I expect they will sometimes.

Every night the two little birds call to their friends and say "Tvit, tvit, tvit!" from the nearby field. I wonder if *you* have heard them. They call so sharply and so loudly that I shouldn't be a bit surprised if you hear them too!

Andrew's robin

In Andrew's garden there was a robin that he called his own. It was a black-eyed, long-legged, red-breasted little bird, so tame that it would take a bit of biscuit from Andrew's fingers.

That summer the robin had built its nest in an old saucepan under the hedge. Andrew remembered putting the saucepan there when he played house, and he had forgotten to take it away. The robin found it, and he and his little wife had put a cosy nest there.

Andrew was pleased. He watched the robins going to and from the nest. He saw the five eggs they laid there. He even saw three of the eggs hatch out. That *was* exciting. The tiny birds inside

the eggs pecked at the shell and broke it. Then out they came – bare black babies without a single feather on them.

The next day all five eggs had hatched. The robins threw the empty shells out of the saucepan nest, and began hunting for caterpillars and grubs to feed their five hungry babies.

"That will keep you busy," said Andrew, as he peeped at the five tiny birds, all with their beaks wide open. "When I dig my garden I will hunt for caterpillars too, and bring them to you."

One day a dreadful thing happened to the robins. A grey squirrel came that way and saw the nest in the saucepan. Now the grey squirrel liked, for a change, to make a meal of baby birds, so when he saw the little robins he ran over to them at once.

The father and mother robin were not there, as they had gone hunting for grubs. The squirrel picked up two of the tiny creatures in his mouth and ran off with them.

How those babies squeaked! The father and mother robin heard them at once and came flying back. When they saw the grey squirrel they knew quite well what he had been up to, and they flew at him, singing loudly in anger, for that is the way of robins.

The squirrel stopped. One robin flew at his right eye and the other flew at his left. He shook his head. He dodged. But it was no use. Those robins would not leave him alone until he dropped the baby birds.

So the grey squirrel dropped them on the lawn, and then bounded off to a tree. Up he went and sat there making faces at the robins.

The robins flew down to their two frightened babies. They were not really hurt – but they could not possibly get back to the nest themselves.

"We must carry them in our beaks," sang the mother robin. But alas! the babies were too heavy.

"Leave them, leave them!" sang the freckled thrush. "I don't bother about my young ones if they fall from the nest."

But the robins were not like the thrush. They would not leave their little ones. But what could they do? The babies were too heavy to carry.

"Fetch Andrew, fetch Andrew!" sang the father robin. "He is kind and strong."

So the robins went to fetch Andrew. He was in the playroom, building a big castle, and was very surprised to see the two robins fly in at the window. The father robin flew to the top of Andrew's big castle and sang loudly to him. Andrew stared at him. The robin flew to the window and back again.

"What is it you want?" asked Andrew, puzzled. The robin sang again and flew to the window-sill. Andrew got up and went too – and he saw something on the lawn. What could it be?

He ran downstairs and out into the garden. As soon as he came to the baby birds, lying helpless on the grass, he guessed why the robins had come to him.

"They want me to put their babies back," said Andrew in delight. "Oh, the clever little things! They knew I would help them."

He gently lifted the two frightened baby birds and took them to the nest in the saucepan. He put them with the others and they soon settled down happily.

"Thank you!" sang the robins. "You are kind!"

The robins were afraid of the squirrel after that. Always one of them stayed to guard the nest until the babies were too big to be taken away by a squirrel. Soon they could fly. Soon they had flown. The little robin family split up, and they all left the garden, except the father robin. This little bird stayed there with Andrew, singing to him as he played in the garden. He never once forgot how kind the little boy had been to the baby birds.

One day Andrew took his clockwork train and lines on to the lawn. He set the train going and had a wonderful time with it. When it was tea-time he had to pack it up in a hurry and go in, and it wasn't till the next day that he found he had lost the key of his beautiful clockwork engine.

"Oh, Mummy, now I can't play with my engine any more, because the key is lost," he said. "I have hunted everywhere in the garden, but I can't find it. I am so unhappy."

The robin heard him. He had seen Andrew winding up the engine. He guessed what the key was – that little shiny thing. He began to hunt for it.

And at last he found it. No wonder Andrew couldn't see it, for it was halfway down a worm's burrow. The robin pulled it out. It was a bit rusty, but it was the lost key, no doubt about that.

The robin took it in his beak and flew to the playroom. He sat on the window-sill and made a little creamy sound, for he couldn't sing very loudly with something in his beak. Andrew looked up.

"Oh!" he cried in great delight. "You've found my key! You dear, good little bird! Thank you so much!"

"You helped me, and I helped you!" carolled the robin. "That is as it should be. Soon it will be winter-time, Andrew. Help me again and give me crumbs."

"I will, I will!" promised Andrew. And I know he will keep his promise.

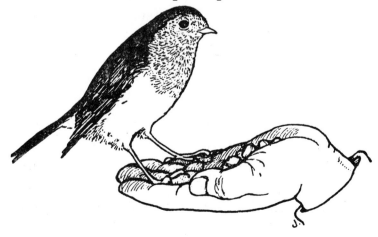

Who would have thought it?

Farmer Gray was a horrid man. He had a bad temper, he was mean and nobody trusted or liked him. He got worse and worse, and at last no one would work for him. Then what a time he and his poor wife had, with the animals to feed, the stables and cowsheds to clean and any amount of other farm jobs to do!

Now one spring a little robin flew into the stable to hunt for a place to make a nest. She flew to a manger – no, that would be dangerous, for her nest might be eaten if she put it there. She flew to an old tin. Yes – that was good – but suppose it got thrown away?

She hunted all around, and at last

she found a very nice place. At least, *she* thought it was. She whistled to her little mate to come and see it. He flew into the stable.

"Look," carolled the hen-robin. "Here is a place for our nest – warm, cosy, the right size and a place not likely to be seen by anyone."

Where do you suppose this place was? In the pocket of Farmer Gray's old brown coat that he had hung up on the wall and forgotten! Well, who would have thought it? The cock-robin looked at the open pocket with bright black eyes.

"Yes," he said to his mate, "it's just the place for us. That pocket will hold all the grass-roots, the leaves and the moss we use, and in this dark stable we shall be safe from weasels, stoats and jackdaws."

So they began to build their nest in the pocket of the farmer's old coat. They made a fine nest. They wove thin grass-roots together, they tucked up the holes with moss and dead leaves, and they found plenty of soft hen-feathers from the farmyard to line the nest softly.

They were very proud of it indeed. Robins always love to nest in anything belonging to humans – and this was a fine place. Soon the hen-robin laid four pretty eggs with red-brown markings. She sat on them day after day. Sometimes the cock took a turn too, so that the hen-robin might stretch her wings. He brought her many tit-bits and sometimes sang a little creamy song to her. They took no notice of the horses stamping in the stable. They got used to the hens coming in and clucking loudly. They were happy and peaceful, looking forward to the hatching of their pretty eggs.

Now one day Farmer Gray got his coat soaking wet in a rainstorm. He took it to his wife and asked her to dry it.

"Oh dear!" she said. "What are you going to wear now? Your other coat

is wet too. What's become of that old brown coat you used to have?"

Farmer Gray frowned. What had he done with it? Ah – he remembered. It was in the stable, of course – it had been hanging there for months!

"It's in the stable," he said. "I'll fetch it."

Off he went. He came to the stable and looked round. "Now where's that coat of mine?" he said.

The hen-robin was sitting on her eggs in the pocket and she heard him. Her small heart beat fast in fright. Oh surely, surely Farmer Gray did not want his old coat now – just when her eggs were due to hatch at any minute! Oh no, no!

The cock-robin was perched nearby. He ruffled up his feathers in fear. What! Take the coat, and crush the nest and break the eggs? Oh no, Farmer Gray! You are a cross, rough man, and nobody likes you – but don't, don't do that!

Farmer Gray saw his coat. "Good! There it is," he said, and went over to it. The cock-robin gave a loud warble and the farmer looked round in surprise. What was the robin singing at *him* for? And then he suddenly knew the answer.

He saw the nest in the pocket of his coat as it hung on the nail. Dead leaves and bits of moss hung out of it. A small hen-robin, her red breast showing up clearly, sat in the pocket on the nest, her anxious black eyes looking trustfully at Farmer Gray.

The farmer looked down at her. He frowned and put out his hand to take the coat. And then he looked into the robin's trustful eyes, and remembered something. He remembered how, when he had been a little boy, a robin had nested in an old boot of his father's, and how delighted he had been – and how sweet the baby robins had looked about the garden. He stood and thought for a minute or two.

"Ah well, you can have my coat," he said to the little robins. "Maybe you need it more than I do!" And with that he went out into the yard without a coat on.

The robins sang for joy. Farmer Gray heard them, and for the first time for years his heart was warm. It was good to be kind to another creature, even if that creature was only a robin. He saw a man going by and he called him. "Hi, John! Come and see here for a minute!"

The man came up in surprise, for it was seldom that Farmer Gray spoke nicely to anyone. The farmer took him to see the robins' nest in his old coat pocket.

"That'll bring you luck, Farmer," said John.

"I need some," said Farmer Gray. "Here's spring come along and I've no one to help me with the farm."

John looked at Farmer Gray and he thought, "Well, here's a man that everyone hates – and yet he's let the robins have his coat. He can't be so bad after all. I've a good mind to come and help him a bit."

"Well, Farmer," he said out loud, "I'll come and give you a hand when I've finished at Farmer Brown's over the hill."

Farmer Gray was pleased. He went to the farm and told his wife about the robins and about how John was going to work for him.

"Those robins will bring me luck," he said, and he laughed. His wife was glad. She had been lonely without any friends to speak to.

John came. He worked hard. He got another man to come. Everything went well. The robins hatched out their eggs, and baby robins fluttered in the old stable. Farmer Gray brought them meal-worms and they grew so tame that they would fly on to his shoulders. How proud Farmer Gray was then! He called all sorts of people in to see his tame robins – and that meant giving them something to eat and drink. Soon the farmer had plenty of friends, and he forgot to frown and grumble.

"Here, my dear. Here's money to buy you a new dress and a new hat," said Farmer Gray to his wife. "We're making money. Things are better. We've got friends to help us. My word! Those robins have brought me luck all right."

"It wasn't really the robins," said his wife. "It was the bit of kindness in your heart, William, that made you spare the robins and their nest. If you had not had that bit of kindness, you would have had no good luck!"

And she was right, wasn't she? We make our own good luck, there's no doubt about that!

The dormouse and the fairy

Once upon a time there was a little fat dormouse with a soft coat and a woffly nose. He was looking for a good place to go to sleep for the cold days of winter – and at last he found one.

It wasn't really a very good place, but the dormouse didn't know that. It was in a greenhouse, inside a plant-pot that was turned on its side. A few dead leaves had blown inside, and it felt warm and cosy there. The dormouse sniffed round a bit and decided that it would be a splendid place for a winter's sleep.

So into the pot he crept, covered himself up with the leaves, put his nose between his front paws, and went soundly to sleep.

The frost came, but it didn't get inside the plant-pot. The snow came, but there was none in the old greenhouse. The little dormouse might have slept there all winter if the gardener hadn't suddenly thought of painting the greenhouse inside and out.

Before he painted it, he tidied it. He took all the pots and saucers and cleaned them. He set them up in rows – and then, as he worked, he came to the one where the little dormouse slept.

He took it up – and he saw the dormouse inside.

"A dozymouse," he said. "Well, I never! Are you the little rascal that nibbles my plants in the spring?"

He shook out the little dormouse, and the poor sleepy little thing woke up with a dreadful jump! Somehow he opened his eyes and made his legs work. Somehow he staggered to a safe corner and hid himself in a hole.

"Oh my! Oh my!" thought the little

dormouse. "This is dreadful! I've been wakened out of my winter sleep. Whatever shall I do? I'd better get out of this greenhouse at once before that gardener finds me and kills me."

So he crawled out of a hole in the wooden side of the greenhouse and ran into the garden.

But it was a bitterly cold winter's day, and the little dormouse felt as if he were freezing. "I shall die – I know I shall!" he said to himself, as he tried to run to and fro to keep himself warm.

Now, as he ran about, he heard a sound of crying. It was a little sound, and was rather like the leaves of trees sighing in a wind. The dormouse listened. It came from the other side of the hedge. He went through the hedge to find out what it was.

And there, curled up on the frosty grass, was a small fairy, not even as big as himself. She had on a dress made of cobwebs, and she was shivering with the cold.

"What's the matter?" asked the dormouse. "Have you been awakened from your winter sleep too?"

"No," said the fairy. "But my warm coat and my warm shawl have been taken away from me. A goblin came along and took them – and he took the blankets from my bed too, and he broke my bed to bits. It was the half of a prickly horse-chestnut case, and was so comfortable. Now I don't know what to do, for I shall freeze to death!"

"Oh no, you won't," said the dormouse, putting a paw comfortingly round her neck. "I'll take care of you. I've been wakened from my winter sleep, and I've nowhere to go either – but we'll look after each other."

"Oh, you poor thing!" cried the little fairy. "Of course, dormice are always asleep in the winter. I quite forgot. Oh dear! You must really find a place to sleep or you will be very ill indeed. Let me help you."

Well, of course, if people help each other they soon manage to do something. The two of them began to hunt for a good place to sleep in – and whatever do you suppose they found? They found an old doll's bed belonging to the little girl who lived in the house near by. It was a very tiny bed indeed, and was very old and rusty. It had belonged to her doll's house, but because it had been left out in the rain and was rusty the little girl had thrown it away on the rubbish-heap. And there it was still, rustier than ever, with no blankets or pillows – but still, a bed.

"I really do prefer a hole of some sort to sleep in," said the dormouse.

"Well, you can't possibly find a hole in all this hard, frosty weather," said the fairy, shivering. "I do wish I could find a coat!"

They put the bed under the hedge and then they set to work to find bedclothes for it. The dormouse knew where there was some moss under the snow, for he remembered it from the summer before. So he scraped away down to it and pulled at it with his mouth. He gave the fairy quite a lot. She was delighted. She borrowed a needle from the fairy tailor, asked a hidden spider for some thread, and made herself a coat of moss and two blankets for the bed. She really was very clever with her needle.

The dormouse found some dead leaves. "They may seem dry and thin to you," he said, "but they are very warm to sleep in. Shall we have them as well in our bed?"

"Oh yes," said the fairy, and from one leaf she made herself a bonnet, and two sheets for the bed. Then the dormouse found some old thistles, still with soft thistledown in their seed-boxes. He pulled out the down and gave it to the fairy. She squealed with delight.

"You really are clever at finding things," she said. "This will do to stuff the pillows and mattress with, and if there's enough I can make an eiderdown too."

There was just enough. So, very soon, there was a soft mattress on the bed, a soft pillow stuffed with thistledown, and an eiderdown made of the skin of some hips, stuffed with the down. Really, it was very cosy indeed.

The sun sank. The world grew bitterly cold. The frost came creeping again over the fields, and the dormouse and the fairy shivered.

"It's time for bed," said the fairy. "Come, dormouse, and see how you sleep in a bed."

She showed him how to climb in under the blankets. Soon his little soft body was lying in bed, and his woffly nose was on the pillow. He felt warm and comfortable. The fairy climbed in beside him and cuddled up to his warm fur.

"You're as good as a hot water bottle!" she said happily. "Oh, it's nice to help one another, isn't it? We would never have found this lovely warm bed if we hadn't made up our minds to work together and help each other. Good night, little dormouse, sleep tight!"

The dormouse was already asleep. And do you know, he is *still* asleep, for the warm days haven't yet wakened him. There he lies in the little bed – but the fairy wakes every day. She is looking for a tiny house for them to live in when he wakes up. She is going to make blue curtains for it. Won't the dormouse be surprised when he opens his eyes and sees it? Mind you don't disturb him if you find him. Just turn back the blanket and have a look at him – then cover him up warmly again, won't you?

The goat, the duck, the goose and the cock

Once upon a time there was a cock who was very tired of living with the hens in his yard, so he made up his mind to run away and find other friends. He set off one morning at dawn, and it wasn't long before he met a fine fat goose, walking along the lane.

"Good morning, Goose," said the cock. "Where are you off to?"

"I have lost my mistress, the goose-girl," said the goose. "I am seeking another mistress now."

"Come with me," said the cock, ruffling out his beautiful tail-feathers. "I am going to see the world."

108

So the goose and the cock walked on together. Presently they came to a little white duck waddling along as fast as her two unsteady legs would carry her.

"Good morning, Duck," said the cock. "Where are you off to?"

"I have heard bad news this morning," said the duck. "The red hen told me that my master was going to kill me for his supper. So I ran away, but I don't know where to go to."

"Come with us," said the cock, standing on his toes, and looking very grand. "We are going to see the world."

So the duck went with the goose and the cock, and they all walked down the lane together till they came to the common.

On the common was a billy-goat, and he had slipped the rope that tied him to his post, and was gambolling about free.

"Good morning," said the cock. "What are you going to do?"

"I don't know," said the goat, joyously. "I am free for the first time in my life – but I don't know where to go."

"Come with us," said the cock, making the red comb on his head stand up very high. "We are going to see the world."

So the goat went with the goose, the duck and the cock, and they all walked over the common together.

"What shall we do?" asked the goat.

"Shall we go to the town of Nottingham and stand by the roadside to beg?" said the cock. "I have a fine voice and I could sing for pennies."

"I could take round the hat," said the duck.

"I could clap my wings in time to your song," said the goose.

"And I could butt anyone who wouldn't give us a penny," said the goat.

So off they set for the town of Nottingham. When they got there it was market day and there were many people about. The four animals stood by

the side of the road, and the cock began to sing:

"Cock-a-doodle-doo,
My baby's lost her shoe,
It had a button blue,
What shall Baby do?"

The goose beat time with her wings, and the duck took round a hat for pennies. The goat stood by ready to butt anyone who would not give them anything.

But before the cock had quite finished his song a burly farmer came up.

"What's all this?" he cried. "Here are four creatures escaped from their pens. Catch them!"

Without waiting a moment the four animals ran away. Through the streets of Nottingham they went and found themselves on the hill outside the town.

"We were nearly caught!" said the goat. "We must not go near a town again. Whatever shall we do?"

"We had better find a cave to live in," said the cock. "See, there is one half-way up the hillside."

"A witch lives there with her ugly daughter," said the duck.

"We will go and ask her if there is another cave near by," said the goose. So off they all went. But when they got to the cave it was empty. No one was there. But there was a cupboard full of good things, and the hungry creatures had a good meal. Then they settled down to sleep.

Now that night the old witch and her daughter returned to the cave. They were a wicked couple, and the people of Nottingham had long tried to get rid of them. The witch stepped into the cave first, and lighted a candle – and the first thing she saw was the table, spread with the remains of the animals' meal.

"Someone has been here!" she cried, and stamped her foot. She and her daughter ran out of the cave and went to a nearby tree to think what they should do. They were afraid that an enemy was in the cave.

"Daughter, you creep back and find out," said the witch. "I will prepare a spell so that if any man or woman is in the cave they cannot harm you. Go."

Now when the witch had shouted and stamped her foot, the four animals had awakened in a fright. The goat was lying near the entrance of the cave, the goose was by the cupboard, the duck was under the table, and the cock was on the back of a chair. They waited to see if anything further would happen – and they heard the witch's daughter coming back.

"It's my mistress!" thought the goat.

"It's my master!" thought the duck.

"It's my mistress!" thought the cock.

"It's the goose-girl!" thought the goose. And all of them were frightened.

The witch's daughter came creeping in. She heard nothing at all. She went to the table and trod on one of the duck's feet underneath.

"Quack-quack, quack-quack-quack!" squawked the duck in pain, and dug his beak into the girl's leg. In a great fright she stumbled towards the cupboard and fell over the goose.

"Ss-ss-ss-ss-sss!" hissed the goose, and struck the witch's daughter with its great wings. Then it began to cackle loudly in fright. The girl was afraid and sat down in a chair trembling. But when she leaned back in the darkness she almost pushed the cock off the back of the chair, and he dug his claws into her hair in terror, crying "Cock-a-doodle-doo! Cock-a-doodle-doo!"

The witch's daughter could not bear it any longer. She fled to the entrance of the cave and fell right over the goat. He butted her so fiercely that she was sent rolling over and over down the hillside and only came to rest under the tree beside the witch.

"What is the matter?" cried the witch. "Didn't my spell work?"

"Oh Mother, oh Mother," said the

daughter, weeping. "The cave is full of powerful wizards. When I went in there was one under the table that cried 'Go back, go back!' And then he stuck a knife into my leg. By the cupboard is a snake that hissed at me in a dreadful manner, and then struck at me with its head. On the back of a chair sits another wizard who cried, 'What a rogue are you! What a rogue are you!' and then nearly pulled my hair out of my head. But worst of all is a giant wizard lying near the entrance. He flung me down the hillside, and here I am."

"What a dreadful thing!" said the witch, trembling. "Our sins have found us out. We must stay here no longer. Come, let us away before dawn."

They hurried off and no one ever heard of them again. As for the four animals, they soon fell asleep and slept peacefully till morning. When they awoke they looked round the cave and were pleased.

"We will live here together," said the cock. "No one will disturb us, for they think that this is a witch's home. We shall be happy here."

They settled down in peace together, and as far as I know, there they may be living still!

Bing-Bong, the paw-reader

F lip and Binkle had been good for a week and three days, and Binkle was beginning to find things very dull.

"Oh!" he groaned, "can't we find a more exciting job than delivering medicine for Sammy Squirrel the chemist? I hate carrying baskets of bottles every day."

Flip preferred to be good. He was afraid of Binkle's exciting ideas; they nearly always led to trouble.

"It's a *very nice* job," he said anxiously. "For goodness sake don't give it up, Binkle."

Binkle put on his cap and opened the door of their home, Heather Cottage.

"Come on!" he said crossly. "I won't

give up the job – not until we get a better one, anyway!"

The two rabbits ran across Bumble Bee Common on their way to Oak Tree Town. When they got there, Binkle saw a big notice pinned up outside Dilly Duck's at the Post Office. He crossed over to look at it. In big letters it said:

A GRAND BAZAAR
WILL BE HELD IN
OAK TREE TOWN

Binkle stroked his fine whiskers and began thinking.

"Come on," said Flip, pulling him next door into Sammy Squirrel's. "Don't dream like that, Binkle. It's time we began work."

But all that day Binkle went on thinking, and hardly said a single word to Flip. In the evening, when Sammy Squirrel paid him, Binkle gave Flip a dreadful shock.

"We shan't be here tomorrow," he said, "so I'm afraid you must get someone else to do the job."

"Oh, Binkle!" cried Flip in dismay. "Whatever do you mean?"

"Sh! I've got a lovely idea!" said Binkle, pulling Flip outside. "Come on, and I'll talk to you about it."

"I don't like your lovely ideas," wailed Flip.

"You'll love this one," said Binkle. "Listen. Did you read that notice about the Bazaar outside Dilly Duck's?"

"Yes," said Flip. "What about it?"

"Well, at the Bazaar there's going to be Bing-Bong, who can read all your life in your paw," said Binkle excitedly. "He'll tell you what's going to happen to you in the future, too."

"Bing-Bong! I never heard of *him*," said Flip. "Anyway, what's it to do with us?"

"Oh, Flip, *can't you guess? One of us will be Bing-Bong*, and read everyone's paws!" said Binkle excitedly.

"Binkle! How can you be so silly?" gasped Flip. "You *know* we can't read paws!"

"Well, we don't need to, silly!" grinned Binkle. "We know all about everyone in Oak Tree Town, don't we? And we can easily tell them all about themselves. They won't know us, for we'll be dressed up, and they'll think we're wonderful!"

"But how can we tell them what will happen in the future?" asked Flip.

"We'll make it up!" said Binkle. "Oh, Flip, what fun it will be!"

"Will it?" said Flip doubtfully. "But look here, Binkle – you're to be Bing-Bong. I don't look a bit like a Bing-Bong person. You do, you're so fat and big, and you've got such lovely whiskers."

Binkle twirled them proudly.

"Yes, I shall be Bing-Bong," he said, "and you can be my assistant. First I must write a note to Herbert Hedgehog, who's putting on the Bazaar."

He sat down and got pen and paper. Presently he showed a letter to Flip. This is what it said:

BING-BONG CASTLE

Dear Sir,

I am Bing-Bong, the reader of paws. I am passing through Oak Tree Town on the day your Bazaar is held. I will call there and read paws.

Yours faithfully,
Bing-Bong.

"There!" said Binkle proudly. "What do you think of that?"

Flip's nose went nervously up and down as he read the letter.

"I *do* hope it will be all right!" he sighed. "You do have such extraordinary ideas, Binkle. I don't know how you think of them."

The letter was sent, and when it reached Herbert Hedgehog he was most excited. He at once arranged to have a little room set apart in Oak Tree Town

Hall for Bing-Bong to sit in and read paws.

"It *will* be grand," he said. "Lots of people will come to the Bazaar now!"

Binkle and Flip were very busy making clothes to wear. Binkle wore a purple suit with a red cloak wound tightly round him. On his head he wore a pointed hat with red stars painted all over it. He looked very grand.

Flip was dressed in baggy trousers and a little black velvet coat. He didn't like them much, for he felt he looked rather silly.

At last the day came, and the two rogues set out over Bumble Bee Common.

"Now remember," said Binkle, "call me Your Highness, and bow before you speak, Flip. You take the money and keep it safe. Leave the rest to me."

Flip wished he could leave *everything* to Binkle, and not go at all, but he didn't dare to say so.

"Oh my! There's Herbert Hedgehog waiting to greet us outside the Town Hall!" he whispered. "Do you think he'll see through our disguise, and know it's us?"

"Of course not!" snapped Binkle, striding forward. Herbert Hedgehog bowed very low when he saw the red-cloaked visitor.

"This is His Royal Highness Bing-Bong!" stammered Flip nervously.

Herbert stood all his prickles up very straight and made way for the two rabbits to go in.

"Very good of you to come, Your Highness," he said, and led the way to the little room at the back of the Hall. "I've made this room ready for you. We shall love to have our paws read by the wonderful Bing-Bong." And he bowed again.

Binkle looked round when Herbert had gone out.

"I'll sit in that big chair," he said. "You stand by the door, Flip. Charge a penny a time, remember."

Very soon there came a timid little knock. Flip swung the door open. Outside stood Creeper Mouse.

"Please, I've come to have my paw read," he said nervously, holding out a penny.

"Your Highness! Someone to have his paw read!" called Flip, beginning to enjoy himself.

Binkle put on some big spectacles and glared at Creeper, who stood tremblingly looking at him. He knew Creeper very well, for he was the postman of Oak Tree Town.

"Come here," commanded Binkle, "and hold out your paw."

Creeper put out his tiny little paw. Binkle stared and stared at it.

"Your paw tells me many things," he said. "It tells me that you have five brothers and sisters. You are married, and you –"

"Oh! oh! oh!" squeaked Creeper, lost in wonder. "How clever you are! It's quite true. Does my paw really tell you that?"

"Of course it does," answered Binkle. "Don't interrupt. It tells me that you walk miles and miles every day carrying a heavy bag."

"Yes, yes, I do," squeaked Creeper. "What's in the bag?"

"Your paw will tell me," said Binkle solemnly, bending closely over it. "Let me see – yes, you carry letters. You are a postman."

"Well, did you ever!" exclaimed the astonished mouse, swinging his tail about delightedly. "Oh, Bing-Bong, please tell me what will happen in my future."

Binkle looked at his paw again. "You will go on a long journey, in a ship," he said gravely. "You will carry letters all your life. You will have twenty-nine children."

"No! no!" shrieked Creeper in horror, snatching his paw away. "Twenty-nine children! Why, how would I feed them all? Oh! oh! Twenty-nine children!"

And he rushed out of the room before Binkle could say another word.

Flip began giggling, but Binkle told him to be quiet.

"*Ssh!*" he said. "Creeper will be telling all the others at the Bazaar, and in a minute they'll all want to come and have their paws read. Listen! There's someone now, Flip."

It was Herbert Hedgehog, holding out his penny and looking rather nervous.

"Creeper Mouse says you're wonderful, Your Highness," he said to Binkle. "Could you read *my* paw, please?"

Binkle looked at it solemnly.

"You live in a yellow cottage," he said. "You grow very fine cabbages."

"So I do – so I do," said Herbert, in the greatest astonishment.

"You have many friends," went on Binkle, "but the two who love you best are –"

"Who?" asked Herbert eagerly,

wondering if they were Dilly Duck and Sammy Squirrel.

"They are – Flip and Binkle Bunny!" said Binkle, now thoroughly enjoying himself.

Flip's nose went up and down in delight, when he saw the astonishment on Herbert's face.

"My best friends!" echoed Herbert. "Flip and Binkle Bunny! Well, well, well! I must be nicer to them in future."

"I *should*," said Binkle, twirling his whiskers very fast, to hide the smile on his face.

"Tell me some more," begged Herbert. "Tell me about the future."

"Er – if you dig up your biggest cabbages, you *may* find a pot of gold underneath," began Binkle.

"Fancy! Oh, my goodness! Oh, excuse me!" begged Herbert, almost stuttering with excitement. "Pray excuse me! I *do* want to go home straight away and see if I can find that gold."

"Oh no, don't do that," shouted Binkle

in alarm . . . but Herbert was gone.

"Bother!" said Binkle in dismay.

"What do you want to go and say such a silly thing for?" demanded Flip in disgust. "You *know* there's no gold under his cabbages."

"*Ssh!* There's someone else," whispered Binkle, as a knock came at the door.

It was Wily Weasel the policeman! Flip almost fell backwards in fright.

"May I have my paw read?" asked Wily politely.

"Oh – er – yes!" stammered Flip, wishing to goodness he could run away.

Wily went up to Binkle and bowed. Binkle took hold of his paw and glared at it. He didn't like Wily Weasel, for Wily had often told him off for being naughty.

"Your paw does not tell me nice things," he began. "It tells me that you are always hunting others and being unkind to them."

"I have to be," said Wily Weasel

cheerfully. "I'm a policeman! There are lots of rogues about Oak Tree Town, and I have to punish them!"

Binkle decided to change the subject. "You are married," he said, "and you love to smoke a pipe."

"Quite right," said Wily, in a pleased voice. "Now tell me about the future. Shall I get rich?"

"*Never!*" said Binkle firmly. "You'll get poorer and poorer. You'll lose your job. You'll be hunted away from Oak Tree Town. You'll be put in prison. You'll –"

"Ow!" yelled Wily in terror, as he listened to all the awful things Binkle was telling. "Don't tell me any more! I don't want to hear anything else!"

He went hurriedly out of the room, groaning and sighing.

"Ooh, I *did* enjoy that," said Binkle. "That's made up for a good deal of trouble I've had from Wily."

Thick and fast came the knocks on the door, and Binkle was as busy as could be, telling everyone about themselves. As he knew all their pasts and made up their futures, he enjoyed himself thoroughly – till in walked someone he *didn't* know!

He was a badger. He held out his paw to Binkle and waited.

"Er – er – er –" began Binkle. "You live far away from here."

"No, I don't," said the Badger. "I live in the next town."

"That's what I meant," cried Binkle. "Er – er – you are married."

"I'm not!" said the badger indignantly. "You don't know what you're talking about! You're a fraud!"

Just at that moment there came a great hubbub outside the door and it burst open suddenly. Herbert Hedgehog came stamping in, followed by a whole crowd of others.

"I've pulled up all the lovely cabbages in my garden," he wailed, "and there's not a piece of gold anywhere! And all my beautiful cabbages are wasted! You're a fraud, Bing-Bong – that's what you are!"

"Yes, he is," cried the badger. "Why, he told me I was married, and I'm not!"

Wily Weasel strode up to Bing-Bong and glared at him.

"Are you Bing-Bong, or aren't you?" he demanded. "Were all those awful things true that you said were going to happen to me – or not?"

"Oh! oh!" wept Flip. "They weren't true, Wily; he made them up, truly he did!"

Wily turned round and looked at Flip. He grabbed off his queer-shaped hat and the green muffler that hid his chin.

"Oho!" he said, "so it's Flip Bunny, is it? And I suppose Bing-Bong is our old friend Binkle?"

Binkle decided to make the best of it.

"Yes," he said, "I'm Binkle. I only came to the Bazaar to give you a bit of fun. I'm sorry about your cabbages, Herbert. Flip, give him the pennies you've got. He can buy some more."

Everyone stared in astonishment at the red-cloaked rabbit. They could hardly believe it was Binkle who had read their paws. They had so believed in him. For a minute everyone felt angry and probably Flip and Binkle would have been punished – if Creeper Mouse hadn't begun to laugh.

"He told me I'd have twenty-nine children," he squeaked. "Oh dear! Oh dear! And I believed him!"

Then everyone began laughing, and even Wily Weasel joined in.

"I'll let you off *this* time," he said to Binkle. "But next time – you just look out! Go off home, both of you. Give Herbert your pennies to buy more cabbages – and don't let me hear any more of you for a *long* time!"

Flip and Binkle scampered off to Heather Cottage as fast as they could go, very thankful to get off so easily.

And for two weeks Binkle had no more lovely ideas.

The dog with the very long tail

There was once a dog with a very long tail. His name was Ginger, because he was just the colour of ginger, and he belonged to little Terry Brown.

Terry was fond of Ginger. He went about everywhere with his dog, and played games with him when he came out of school. Ginger loved Terry too, and would have done anything in the world for him. His tail never stopped wagging when he was with Terry.

One day Terry was very excited. There was to be a grand garden party in the Rectory garden, with sweet-stalls, competitions, baby shows

and dog shows. Terry was going, and he made up his mind to buy some peppermint sweets and to have a bottle of ginger beer and two dips in the bran-tub.

"There's to be a maypole dance too," he told his mother, "and I shall watch that. Mr Jones is having a coconut shy, and I shall have two tries at that."

"Well, I will give you fifty pence to spend," said his mother. "That should be plenty for everything, Terry."

"Oh, thank you," said Terry. "I shall take Ginger with me and buy him a bar of chocolate. He'll love that."

When the day came Terry and Ginger walked to the garden party. Terry had the fifty pence piece in his pocket, and he was planning all he would do with it. He looked round the grounds and decided that he would start with a go at the coconut shy. He thought it would be lovely to win a big nut.

"I'll have a go," he said to the man. "How much?"

"Three balls for five pence," said the man. Terry put his hand into his pocket to get his money – and, oh dear me – it was gone! There was a hole at the bottom and the fifty-pence piece had dropped out!

Terry was so upset. He went back to look for his money but he couldn't find it anywhere. Ginger went with him and was just as upset as his master.

"Now I can't buy any sweets or ginger beer, or have any dips in the bran-tub," said poor Terry, sadly. "All my money is gone. Oh, Ginger, I do think it's bad luck, don't you?"

Ginger pushed his nose into Terry's hand and looked up at him with big brown eyes. He was very sorry for his master. He thought he would go and look for the lost money by himself, so he trotted off, nose to ground, trying to find the silver coin.

Suddenly Ginger came to where a great many dogs were all gathered together with their masters and mistresses, and he ran up to a collie dog called Rover, a great friend of his.

"What are you all doing here?" he asked Rover.

"Waiting for the dog shows," answered Rover.

"I hope you win a prize," said Ginger.

"Aren't you going in for the show?" asked Rover.

"No," said Ginger, wagging his tail. "My little master, Terry, is very sad. He has just lost all his money and I'm looking for it."

Just at that moment the dog show began, and the dogs moved into the ring. Ginger stayed to watch. It was a comic dog show, and there were prizes for the fattest dog, the thinnest dog, the dog with the saddest eyes, and the dog with the shortest legs. Ginger thought it was very funny.

"Now then!" cried the man who was running the dog show. "Which dog has the longest tail! Come along, everybody! I've got a measuring tape here to measure the tails with! Bring in your dogs! The one with the longest tail gets fifty pence!"

Now when Ginger heard that, a fine plan suddenly came into his head! Surely no dog had a longer tail than his! Everybody laughed at his tail because it was so very long. He would trot into the ring and show it to the judge!

So Ginger pushed his way through the people watching and trotted into the ring, where other dogs stood having their tails measured.

Ginger went right up to the judge and stuck his tail out to be measured.

"Ha!" cried the judge. "Here is a dog who thinks his tail is quite the longest! Stand still, Dog, and let me measure it!"

All the people laughed and Ginger stood quite still while the judge measured his tail.

"My goodness, what a long one!" he cried. "Why, it's two feet long! Little dog, I think you must have the prize! Who is the owner of this dog? Will he please step forward and take the prize?"

Now Terry happened to be peeping at the dog show at that moment and he was most astonished to see his dog, Ginger, trot into the ring and hold up his tail to be measured. He was still more surprised to hear that Ginger had won a prize, and he stepped into the ring to take it for him.

"Fifty pence!" said the judge, and he gave a nice bright silver coin to Terry. Then he patted Ginger and the grateful dog licked his hand.

"Good old Ginger!" said Terry, running off with him. "Fancy you thinking of putting yourself in for the longest-tailed dog! I know why you did it, Ginger! You did it because you were sorry that I had lost my money! You're the cleverest, dearest dog in the world, and I'm going to buy you a bun, two biscuits and a stick of chocolate!"

Ginger wagged his long tail and barked for joy. He bounded along by Terry and when his little master had bought him all that he had said he would, he wagged his long tail quite two hundred times a minute.

"Wuff, wuff!" he said, and he ate up the bun, the biscuits, and the chocolate in one gulp!

"Good old Ginger!" said Terry. "Now come along to the coconut shy! I'll see if I can't get a coconut *this* time!"

Off they went – and Terry knocked down the largest coconut of the lot! Wasn't he lucky? Then he went to buy some sweets and some ginger beer, and had three dips in the bran-tub – all with Ginger's fifty pence; and you may be sure there wasn't a prouder dog than Ginger at the garden party that day!

Paddy the puppy

Alan was staying with his Auntie Betty and his cousin Jenny. He liked it very much except that Auntie Betty was much stricter than his own mother!

She made him wipe his feet properly and hang up his things as soon as he took them off. "If you throw them down on the floor again you won't have any cake for tea!" she told him – and when he forgot, she kept her word and he *didn't* have cake for tea! He sulked, and Cousin Jenny laughed at him.

There was a lovely big garden to play in, and Jenny had a little bicycle and a tricycle too, so they had some fine racing. There was a swing to swing on

and a sandpit to play in, so there was
always plenty to do.

"Remember to bring in your toys
when you come in!" Auntie Betty said.
Jenny always remembered and Alan
always forgot! Then out he had to go
and collect them all.

"Remember to shut the gate when

you go out in case the puppy runs out and gets run over," said Auntie Betty, each morning. And again, Jenny always remembered, and Alan always forgot!

Auntie Betty was cross then. "Don't you *like* the puppy, Alan?" she would say. "Don't you care enough for the little thing to remember to shut the gate? You are unkind!"

"I *do* like him," said Alan. "I love him. He's a darling and I do love the way he wags his tail and comes running to meet me. I *will* remember to shut the gate."

"If anything happens to Paddy because of you, I'll never, never forgive you!" said Cousin Jenny. "You don't even *try* to remember things! I think you must have a very poor sort of brain."

"I *haven't*!" said Alan, at once. "My mother says I'm going to be clever. I've nearly been top at school three times!"

"Well, you're not clever *now!*" said Jenny. "Who left his toys out in the rain yesterday again? Who didn't . . ."

"Be quiet!" said Alan, sulkily. "I tell you I'm going to remember everything from now on!"

Certainly that day he was quite good at remembering all he had been told. He even remembered to shut the door quietly after him instead of slamming it. Auntie Betty was surprised!

"We shall send you back home a different boy!" she said. "Your mother will be pleased!"

Jenny and Alan were sent out next day to buy a collar and a lead for little Paddy the pup.

"He's growing now," said Auntie Betty. "He must learn to wear a collar, and to walk nicely on the lead."

"Can I take him out for a walk and teach him?" said Jenny. "Do let me!"

"Well – you're a very sensible little girl, so perhaps I'll let you!" said her mother.

"Can *I* take Paddy too?" asked Alan at

once. "I'm sensible as well."

"You're not," said Jenny. "You'd lose Paddy or let him get run over or something! He can't be trusted with Paddy, can he, Mummy?"

"We'll see," said her mother. "Anyway, you go and buy him a collar and lead this morning."

Paddy wasn't very pleased with his new collar, and he didn't like the lead at all! When Jenny put it on him and tried to walk him round the garden, he pulled away from her, and tried to escape.

"Oh, Paddy – you're nearly pulling my arm out!" said Jenny. "Walk to heel, and don't drag in front all the time."

"Let *me* take him," said Alan. "I'm a boy and boys' arms are stronger than girls'! I can soon teach him."

It was true that Alan was very good with Paddy. He was very patient and kind, and soon the puppy began to understand what it was that he was supposed to do.

"There you are!" boasted Alan. "I told you I could soon teach him!"

And then, at that very moment, Paddy gave a sudden jerk at the lead, pulled it out of Alan's hand, and ran to the front gate, where he had just seen a doggy friend pass by. The gate was open and the puppy frisked out into the road. A car hooted suddenly and swerved.

"Oh Paddy! He's out in the road!" cried Jenny and ran to get him. Her mother heard the car's hoot and looked out of the window. She was cross when she saw the puppy in the road.

"Who left that front gate open?" she called. And, of course, as usual it was Alan. He went very red in the face. "I did. I'm so sorry. I just came running in and swung it behind me, thinking it would shut all right," he said.

Jenny was hugging the puppy, glaring at her cousin angrily. "He nearly got run over! All because of you! Do you know what I would have done if he had been hurt? I would

150

have thrown all your toys out of the window, and smashed your engine, and I would have told your mother to fetch you home, and – "

"That's enough, Jenny," said her mother. "You may be sure that if Alan does anything really bad *I* will deal with him and take him home, not you! Please do try and keep your temper!"

"I've said I was sorry, Jenny," said Alan.

"It isn't *enough* to be sorry – always to be sorry, sorry, sorry!" cried Jenny. "Why can't you be sensible? Then you wouldn't *have to be sorry!*"

Alan really did try to remember everything properly for the next two days. He was very good with the puppy too, and taught him a great deal. In fact, Paddy was soon walking beautifully on the lead, his nose just touching Alan's heels as he padded along.

"I can take Paddy for a walk, Mummy says," said Jenny next day. "Not with you. Only by myself."

"Oh, well, can *I* take him for a walk too, by *myself*?" said Alan. "Auntie, can I?"

"Yes," said his Aunt. "Jenny can take him this morning and you can take him this afternoon."

Jenny took Paddy off proudly, the lead fastened to his nice new collar. When she came back she told her mother that Paddy hadn't *really* been very good.

"He kept wanting to talk to all the other dogs he met," she said. "And sometimes I had to *drag* him away, and that's bad for his neck."

"You could have carried him then," said Alan. "That's what *I* shall do if I have any bother with him this afternoon. But I think he'll be very good with me."

Alan set out with Paddy after dinner. The little dog was delighted to have another walk. He trotted off at Alan's heels, as good as gold.

Alan talked to him all the way and

Paddy listened. "When you are with two-legged people, you don't stop and talk to *four*-legged creatures," Alan explained to him. "That's bad manners. But if *I* stop and talk, you just sit down politely and wait."

Paddy listened and behaved very well indeed. Then he suddenly pricked up his ears, and so did Alan. "Drums! Trumpets! There's a band coming!" he said. "I'll just tie you to this railing, Paddy, and go and stand at the kerb and watch. Sit there, like a good dog!"

Alan ran to the kerb to see the band pass. Rum-tiddy-rum, BOOM-BOOM-BOOM, tan-tan-tan-tara, BOOM! It was a wonderful band, and not only the soldiers were marching in time, but all the passers-by too! Some children came along, marching in a row, and called to Alan.

"Come on – this is fun!"

Alan joined in, and marched with the others, left-right, left-right, boom-diddy-boom, diddy-diddy-boom, boom, BOOM!

He went all the way with the soldiers till they came to their camp and went in through the gate. Then he turned to go home.

But before he had gone very far he remembered something. "Oh – PADDY! I left him tied up. Goodness me – I forgot all about him. Poor little puppy!"

He raced back to the railings to untie the puppy – but to his horror Paddy was gone. Alan stood and stared and then he looked up and down the road. Somebody must have stolen Paddy! He couldn't have got free by himself!

He ran to a woman standing outside a greengrocer's shop, serving her customers. "Oh please – did you see anyone take a puppy away a few minutes ago? He was tied to those railings."

"A puppy? Yes, I heard him whining," said the woman. "And when I looked

round I saw a girl taking his lead from the railing-spike, and leading him away."

"Oh! The wicked girl!" cried Alan. "What was she like? I'll go and tell a policeman!"

"Well – she seemed quite ordinary," said the woman, surprised. "She had on a blue dress with yellow stripes and a blue hat with yellow flowers, and sandals. That's all I remember."

Alan saw a policeman standing at a nearby corner and ran to him. "Please!" he said. "Someone's stolen my puppy. I left him over there for a minute – and a girl in a blue dress with yellow stripes took him away."

"Now, don't you upset yourself," said the policeman, opening his notebook. "Give me your name and address, and the dog's name – and I'll soon make enquiries. Don't you worry!"

Alan felt dreadful. How could he have forgotten little Paddy? Jenny was right, he must have a poor sort of brain.

He loved Paddy. He couldn't bear to think anything had happened to him. Whatever would Jenny say – and Auntie Betty?

"Jenny said she'd throw all my things out of the window!" he remembered. "She said she'd tell my mother and I'd be sent home. How can I go and say I've lost Paddy? I daren't. I simply daren't!"

He decided to go back to his aunt's, slip in at the back door, and go up to pack his things. He would go home to his mother and tell her what a failure he was – he had even lost the puppy he loved! He wouldn't tell Jenny and his aunt what had happened – he wouldn't even see them.

He ran back to the house and slipped in at the back door. No one was about. He went upstairs, found all his toys and clothes and packed them into his bag. Then he crept downstairs, meaning to catch the bus.

And *just* as he tried to slip out of the back door, who should come in but his aunt! How surprised she was to see Alan stealing out with his suitcase!

"Why – whatever are you doing? Where are you going?" she said. And then Alan burst into tears, though he knew it was a babyish thing to do.

"I lost Paddy!" he wailed. "I tied him to a railing and followed a band, and forgot him. And when I got back he wasn't there. A girl came and stole him!"

"Oh, Alan!" said his aunt.

"I told a policeman!" said Alan, wiping his eyes. "I hope he'll put that girl into prison. She's wicked. But I'm wicked too, to forget Paddy."

Suddenly there came a knock at the front door. Auntie Betty went to open it. Outside stood the policeman – and with him were Jenny – and Paddy! A most excited Paddy who flung himself on Alan at once and licked him all over.

"Why – what's this!" said Auntie Betty.

"Mother, this policeman stopped me and said Paddy wasn't mine!" cried Jenny. "I suddenly saw him tied up to a railing all by himself, and he was whining so loudly that I couldn't bear it. Alan wasn't anywhere about – so I guessed he had forgotten Paddy and I untied him and took him shopping with me."

"Er – well – it seems that a bit of a mistake has been made," said the policeman, smiling. "Ah, there's the boy who reported to me that the dog was stolen – stolen by a girl in a blue dress with yellow stripes, he said – so, of course, when I saw this young lady dressed like that, *and* with a dog, well, I had to find out what was happening!"

"You'd better take that boy to prison!" said Jenny, pointing at poor Alan. "He's a bad, wicked boy!"

"Don't be silly, Jenny," said her mother. She thanked the policeman, then said goodbye to him and shut the front door. "Look – Alan is so upset about everything that he has packed his bag and wants to go home. Shall we let him?"

Jenny stared at Alan's red eyes, and watched Paddy trying to comfort him. "I shan't ever forget things again – not after this," said Alan, in a low voice, stroking Paddy's soft head. "If you could just trust me once more . . ."

"All right," said Jenny. "I'll forgive you – but only because Paddy does, see? I don't *really* want you to go home."

So Alan unpacked his bag again and stayed. "You've taught me a lesson, Paddy," he told the puppy. "I've taught *you* plenty of things – and you learnt them well. Now you've taught *me* something, and I'll learn that well too. Do you understand?"

"Wuff!" said Paddy. Yes – of *course* he understood!

The thrush and his anvil

It was a lovely spring morning. The birds were singing, and the sun shone into Jane's room so brightly that she woke up early and jumped out of bed without waiting for her mother to come and call her.

"I must go out and see how my plants are getting on," she thought. "We have had so many wet days lately that I have not been out in the garden for quite a long time. I'll go before breakfast, while it is fine."

She dressed quickly and ran out into the garden. The air smelt warm and moist after the rain. Jane had a little piece of garden of her own which she looked after with special care, and she hoped to find that her plants had grown quite big.

So they had, but, oh dear! nearly every leaf had a piece bitten off it! Jane was most upset. She ran round the rest of the garden, and found that Daddy's plants were just the same. Lots of his young lettuces were eaten too.

She rushed back to the house and burst into the dining room where Mummy, Daddy, and Peter were sitting down to breakfast.

"Daddy," she cried, "something is eating all our young plants! Something big too – not just a caterpillar or a grub."

"It's probably the snails," said Daddy. "After all, they have about fourteen thousand teeth on their tongues you know. They can do a lot of damage in one night! And there are generally a lot of them about after rain."

"Gracious – have snails got teeth on their tongues?" said Peter. "I never knew that. Fourteen thousand teeth –

why, their tongues must be like rasps, then!"

"They are," said Daddy, "like files. Of course, they are not the kind of teeth you and I have, Peter! But they are very strong, and a snail can eat most of a young plant in a night, using his ribbon-tongue."

"But doesn't he wear it out?" asked Jane.

"Yes, but it is always growing," said Daddy.

"Well, what are we to do about our snails?" asked Jane. "We can't let them eat everything in the garden. There must be dozens of them about."

"Finish your breakfast," said Daddy, "and then we will go and look at the damage."

They were soon out in the garden and looking at the plants.

Suddenly Daddy stopped and pointed to something.

"Hallo!" he said. "We needn't worry much about your plague of snails.

Somebody else knows about them and is dealing with them. See that stone? That is the thrush's anvil – the place he comes to when he has caught a snail and wants to smash its shell."

The children saw a flint beside the path. Round it were scattered many fragments of broken shell.

"Did the thrush really have the sense to come and use this stone for an anvil?" said Peter, half doubtful.

"Well, come into the summer-house here and we'll watch," said Daddy. "It's always better to see a thing for yourself than to hear about it second-hand. Come on."

They sat down in the summer-house and waited. They didn't have to wait long. Soon a thrush with a freckled breast flew down to the stone.

"He's got a snail in his beak!" whispered Jane.

So he had. Then he began to deal with the snail. He struck it hard on the stone anvil again and again.

Tap, tap, tap, tap! Tap, tap, tap, tap!

"I've often heard that noise before and I didn't know what it was!" whispered Peter. "Now I shall know it's a thrush using his anvil!"

The thrush worked hard. The snail-shell was strong and it wouldn't break. The thrush beat it down with all his might. Crack!

"It's broken!" said Jane. "Now he can get at the soft body inside. He's eating the snail, Daddy."

"Poor snail!" said Peter. "But he shouldn't eat our lettuces!"

"Clever thrush!" said Daddy, getting up. "Well – I think you can leave him to deal with your snails, don't you?"

Shellyback the tortoise

William and Susie had a tortoise. They called him Shellyback because his back was just a big hard shell, and they liked him very much. He wandered about all over the garden and ate the grass and any rose petals that he could find. He also ate some of Daddy's lettuces and some nice young pansy plants, which made Daddy very cross indeed.

Now, when Daddy had bought Shellyback, the man who was selling him had told Daddy that Shellyback would be most useful in the garden, and would eat up all the slugs and the beetles and caterpillars. So Daddy had been pleased, and was sure Shellyback

would be a good friend.

But tortoises eat green things, not insects, which they don't like at all, so Daddy found that Shellyback wasn't so useful in the garden after all. But, as Susie said, it wasn't poor Shellyback's fault that the man who had sold him told Daddy an untruth.

"I think we'll get rid of that tortoise," Daddy said when he found that some of his lettuces had been eaten. "He's no use at all."

"But, Daddy, we like Shellyback," said William. "Really, we do. He puts his head out of his shell when we come along and looks at us so nicely out of his little brown eyes. He is a friendly creature."

"Well, I'll give him another chance," said Daddy.

So Shellyback was allowed to wander about the garden again, and William and Susie watched to see that he did no damage. They got some wire and made him a little patch of grass of his own. They gave him a handful of rose petals, because he seemed to like those more than anything else. There old Shellyback lived in the sunshine, and seemed very happy indeed.

Then one autumn day he escaped and went into Daddy's seed-bed. Daddy had some nice young delphinium plants, all ready to plant out next year. He was very proud of them – and dear me,

Shellyback was very foolish indeed, for he chose just those to nibble right down to the ground.

When William and Susie got home from school they hunted for Shellyback, and when they found what he had done they were most alarmed.

"Daddy will certainly make us give him away now," said William. "Those delphiniums were his favourite plants. Oh, dear! Shellyback, you really are silly!"

The next day was Saturday. Daddy was going to spend it gardening. He went out happily into the garden and took his spade. It was good to be out in the sunshine even though the wind was frosty cold.

Daddy dug till he was tired, and then he went indoors to get his pipe. He put his hand into his pocket to get out his matches, and discovered that his key, which he kept in the same pocket, had gone. He must have dropped it whilst he was in the garden.

"Oh, bother!" said Daddy. "That's the key of the office safe. If I lose that it is a serious matter. I shan't be able to open the safe on Monday morning. William and Susie, you must help me to look for it in the garden."

"All right, Daddy," said William. "Where do you think you may have dropped it?"

"Anywhere, almost," said Daddy. "I've been nearly all over the garden this morning. The key may have fallen out of my pocket on to the path, or on the grass, or in the beds."

"Have you been in your young delphinium bed today?" asked Susie.

"No, why?" asked Daddy.

"Well, Daddy, we are sorry but Shellyback went there yesterday and ate your young plants." said Susie.

"What!" cried Daddy angrily. "He ate those lovely delphiniums of mine – the ones I grew from seed myself and have been watching so carefully all the summer? I said that tortoise must go and now he certainly must. He's a most destructive creature!"

Daddy jumped up and went striding out of doors to his young plants. When he saw his nice delphiniums nibbled right down to the roots he roared with rage.

"Where's that tortoise? I'll give him away to the milkman or the butcher or somebody this very day."

The children looked ready to cry. They knew that Shellyback certainly *would* go now.

"Go and fetch that tortoise and bring him here," said Daddy.

So off went William and Susie, but when they got to Shellyback's patch he wasn't there! He had pushed himself under the wire netting and had gone off somewhere.

They ran back to Daddy. "He's gone," they said.

"Gone?" said Daddy. "Well, he's probably eating something else of mine, then! Find him! And just hunt for my key at the same time."

The children hunted everywhere for Shellyback. They hunted under the bushes; they hunted under the hedge at the bottom of the garden; they even hunted indoors. But nowhere could the tortoise be seen. He had quite disappeared.

"Have you found him?" asked Daddy.

"No," said Susie. "We think he must have run away, Daddy. We've hunted everywhere."

"I expect he guessed he'd better make himself scarce," said Daddy. "Eating my plants like that! Now, help me to hunt for my key. I simply *must* find that."

Well, they hunted and they hunted for the key. But that key didn't seem to be anywhere in the garden. Like the tortoise, it had completely disappeared. Daddy was very upset.

"We must look again tomorrow," he said when the evening came and it was no use hunting any more. "I really must have it by Monday, or I may get into serious trouble at the office."

The children went to bed feeling sad. They didn't want Daddy to get into trouble, and they were unhappy because Shellyback had disappeared too. Things had gone very wrong that day!

The next day William and Susie went to the kitchen garden to see if there were any lettuces left for a salad. As they walked round it, they saw the place where Daddy had been digging the day before. The earth looked fresh and was dug very neatly, for Daddy was a good gardener.

As William looked along the earth, he saw something strange. He stopped and looked again.

"Susie," he said, "does it seem to you as if the earth is moving just over there? Look!"

He pointed, and Susie looked. She stared in surprise. The earth certainly *was* moving. It was just like a very tiny earthquake going on in one corner.

"How funny!" said Susie. "What can it be?"

"We'd better go and see," said William. So they ran to look. The earth was heaving here and there, and little bits came up into the air every now and again.

"It's some creature burying itself," said Susie. "Whatever is it?"

William fetched a spade, and very carefully dug all round the heaving earth. And then he saw what was burying itself. Guess what it was!

"It's Shellyback the tortoise!" cried Susie in astonishment. "He's burying himself. Oh, how funny! I didn't know tortoises buried themselves, did you, William? Had we better get him out, do you think?"

Just then their next-door neighbour, Miss White, looked over the wall, and they told her what was happening.

Miss White knew all about tortoises.

"Oh, yes," she said. "They always bury themselves in the ground in the winter because they don't like the cold, you know. They like to go to sleep all the winter through and wake up in the spring. If I were you I'd get him carefully out of the hole he has dug for himself and put him in a box of earth. If you leave him in the ground, Daddy may come along with his spade and crack his shell by accident when he digs over the bed. He will sleep in the box till the spring and wake up again then. Put him into a shed and he will be quite all right."

"I'm afraid Daddy is going to give him away," said Susie sadly. "But still, we'd better dig him up."

So, very carefully, the children took up old Shellyback – and as they wiped away the earth from his shell, something bright fell to the ground. William picked it up and stared at it in surprise.

"Daddy's key!" he cried. "Look, Susie,

it's Daddy's lost safe key! Oh, won't he be pleased?"

"Shellyback found it!" said Susie. "Shellyback found it! If it hadn't been for him we wouldn't have seen it. It would have lain in the ground for ever. Come and tell Daddy."

Leaving the tortoise where he was, the children raced indoors to Daddy.

"Daddy! Daddy!" they shouted. "Here's your key! Look! It was in the bit of garden that you dug over yesterday. It must have fallen out when you were digging there."

Daddy was delighted. "Oh, good!" he said. "Thank you very much, children. I am so pleased to have my key again. I know how hard you have looked for it. I would like to give you a little reward. What would you like?"

Susie and William looked at each other. They both thought of the same thing – Shellyback!

"Daddy," said William, "*we* didn't find the key, really – Shellyback did!"

"Shellyback! But I thought he had gone," said Daddy. "You said you couldn't find him."

"He *had* gone," said Susie. "He had gone to bury himself for the cold winter, and the hole he dug up was where you had dropped your key, Daddy. So when we brushed the dirt off the tortoise, your key fell to the ground."

"Well, well, well!" said Daddy.

"So, Daddy, as Shellyback found your key for you, do you think you could let us still keep him?" asked William. "Miss White says he will sleep all through the winter in a box, so he won't do any more damage now – and we will promise to make his patch so strong with wire-netting next year that he can't possibly escape to eat your plants."

"Well, you seem to have made up your minds to keep Shellyback," said Daddy; "and as he really does seem to have found my key for me, I'll reward him – and you too. You may keep him."

"Oh, thank you, Daddy!" cried the two children, and they hugged Daddy hard.

Then they ran off to find a nice box for Shellyback. They put him in, with some earth at the bottom, and carried him in the box to the shed. They put him on a shelf there, and he is sleeping soundly, quite comfy and safe in his box.

The lost baby mouse

There was once a little mouse who was far too daring. He ran out of his hole at any time of the day or night, and his mummy was very cross with him.

"One of these days you will get caught by the cat," she said.

"Oh, I'm too quick for the cat!" the little mouse said, and he twitched his whiskers to and fro in a way that made his mummy very angry.

"Don't make faces at me!" she cried, crossly. The little mouse gave a squeak and ran right out of his hole. Luckily for him the cat was not there, or that would have been the end of him. The hole led out into the kitchen, and there were often crumbs and scraps of food to

be found on the floor.

The little mouse hunted round for some, but there were none because the cook had swept them all up. "Well, I'll look round the world a bit and see what I can find somewhere else," thought the little mouse. So he ran out of the kitchen door into the hall.

He came to the stairs. He saw the first step – and the second step – and the third step – good gracious, it seemed to him as if these enormous stairs must lead up to the sky!

"Now I've heard that the moon is made of green cheese," said the baby mouse to himself, "and if so it would be a wonderful place to live. These great big steps must surely lead up to the moon. Tails and whiskers, how high up they go!"

The mouse began to climb them one by one. It seemed a very long way up to him. But at last he reached the very, very top. There was a landing at the top, and four or five doors led off it. The mouse ran into the nearest one.

It was the playroom where the children had all their toys, and played happily together. The mouse was very frightened to see a bear, a horse, a dog, an elephant, and a pink rabbit staring at him.

"Oh, pardon me!" he said, trying to back out of the door quickly. "I didn't know this was the zoo."

The teddy bear laughed so much that he couldn't speak. So the pink rabbit spoke up.

"Of course it's not the zoo, silly. We are only toys."

But the mouse had gone in a fright. He ran to another door. A bedroom was behind that, cold and empty. All the other doors were shut.

And then the cat appeared! My goodness! It came stalking round the corner of the landing, tail in air, green eyes gleaming!

The mouse gave a squeak of fright.

He ran into the playroom, with the cat after him. The cat pounced – and the baby mouse's tail was scratched with the cat's big claws. It dashed into an open brick-box and the teddy bear neatly shut the lid on him!

"Ssssss!" hissed the cat at the bear. But she didn't like his staring glass eyes and she turned and went out of the door again.

"She's gone," said the bear, opening the box. "Are you hurt, Baby Mouse?"

"My tail is bleeding," wept the poor little creature. "Oh, whatever am I to do? I am quite, quite lost. I was looking for the moon up here to have a good feast of green cheese – but it didn't seem to be anywhere."

"You won't find the moon up here, Baby Mouse. Hasn't your mummy ever told you about the playroom? We see her sometimes when the children take us downstairs," said the pink rabbit kindly. "I say, where's Angela the doll? She knows how to put bandages on.

Angela! Come over here and see to this dear little mouse."

Angela came up. She was a beautiful blue-eyed doll, with thick curly hair. She loved the tiny mouse as soon as she saw him. She made the pink rabbit fetch some water out of the goldfish bowl on the bookshelf to bathe the mouse's tail.

He climbed up with a dish out of the doll's house, and soon came back carrying the water very carefully.

"Good rabbit," said Angela. "Put the bowl down there. Get the sponge out of the doll's house bathroom."

There was the tiniest sponge imaginable in the bathroom, and the rabbit fetched it. Soon Angela was bathing the mouse's tail. Then she tore her tiny white handkerchief in half and bound it neatly round the little tail.

"Oh, thank you," said the mouse, gratefully. "I do think you are kind. What shall I do now? Is there a mouse hole anywhere in this playroom? I could go down it and live there. I shall never, never dare to go out of this room in case I meet the cat."

"Well, there isn't a mouse hole," said the pink rabbit. "We've often and often looked, little mouse. I suppose you wouldn't like to live in the brick-box?"

"No, thank you," said the mouse. "It's not very comfortable – and the children might tip me out with the bricks."

"True," said the bear. All the toys thought hard – and then the pink rabbit gave a squeal and clapped his fat paws together.

"I know!" he cried. "Why can't the baby mouse live in the doll's house? Nobody lives there at all, because the children took all the little dolls out to live in the toy farmyard and look after the animals there. The baby mouse is just small enough."

"Oh, that *is* a good idea!" cried everyone. "Come along, Mouse – we'll take you in at the front door."

So they all trooped across to the doll's house, and the teddy knocked on the little brass knocker. Of course there was nobody to answer, so they just pushed open the door. Only the mouse was small enough to go in at the door, and he ran into the tiny hall in delight.

"Oh, it's lovely!" he cried. "Really lovely! Look at the tiny stairs! Are there bedrooms above?"

"There is one bedroom and a tiny bathroom," said the rabbit, looking in at the window. "Here, Mouse, take the sponge and put it back again in the bathroom. And you can have a bath if you like."

Well, the baby mouse had a wonderful time. He filled the bath with water by turning on the tiny tap. He got into it and washed with the bit of soap there. He got out, stood on the teeny-weeny bath mat and dried himself with the towel. He did feel nice and clean after that.

"I feel dreadfully tired," he called to the toys, who were all peeping in at the windows, watching the mouse with joy. "Do you think I might sleep in this bed? It's just big enough for me. Would it matter if I got under the blankets do you think? I love to be cosy."

"Oh, *do* get into the bed!" cried the doll. "I will put my arm in at the window and tuck you up. You will look really sweet."

So the baby mouse got into the tiny doll's bed, and the big doll put her arm in through the open window and tucked him up. Just his ears, pointed nose, and whiskers showed above the sheet. He shut his eyes and in half a minute he was fast asleep.

All the toys came to peep at him, even the old plush monkey who was so bad-tempered that nobody liked playing with him. Everyone loved looking at the baby mouse asleep in the doll's tiny bed.

"He can live here as long as he likes," said Angela the doll. "He can have his meals in the kitchen off the little table. We will teach him good manners. He can keep the house clean, and sometimes, for a treat, he can cook us some tiny cakes on the stove. We've always wanted to use the doll's house stove, but we are all too big to go inside the kitchen door! Next time the children take me downstairs, I will tell his mummy that he is quite safe with us."

So the baby mouse lived in the doll's house, and felt quite safe there if the cat happened to come into the playroom. Once the cat came and looked in at the doll's house window, and the mouse sat on the kitchen table and made faces at her. Angela said he shouldn't have done that because it was bad manners.

"But I did so like making faces at the cat," said the mouse. "Really I did. Oh, toys, I'm so glad I came to your playroom. I do so love my little house. The only thing is – how I wish one of you was small enough to come and have tea with me!"

And now the little mouse has got his wish! A clockwork mouse has come to live with the toys – and today the real mouse is having the clockwork mouse to tea! Wouldn't you love to peep in at a window and see them both sitting in the kitchen together? I would!